# RUTH

request appeared in the family basket along with regular provisions, and Stores professed abundance: most sane requests were met.

The insane requests came from children, who desired chocolate and bubble gum without pretense. Stores banked these wishes for birthday baskets and Christmas presents, which it emitted with alarming canniness, ignoring only the lazily forged; it was unlikely that Ruth's mother had asked for the six rolls of "duck" tape petitioned in her name.

THE AMISH APPLES WEIGHED HEAVILY UPON RUTH'S MOTHER. Esther Scholl could no more let them go bad than she could throw away string or tinfoil; she was the wife of the community's Steward, and, as such, obligated to offer final home to all that he acquired, even in error. These seven barrels, the fruit of her husband's thrift, had been rendered in lieu of payment from the Amish settlement in Gladwin to whom the community had sold an old draft saddle, and sat like a paperweight on her brain until she was sure each would be put to use. Esther had nimble Colony hands that could core and peel an apple without looking. Ruth sat on her lap, mesmerized, while her mother chatted with Cynthia.

Cynthia had been sent to support the Scholls. As an aging single sister, she was unlikely ever to run her own household, but installed in Ruth's, she assumed strange powers, the stranger for her Colony habits: the particular dirge she hummed while combing hair, her refusal to enter rooms with ceiling fans. Cynthia was allowed to cook with the family's food and to wipe the children's faces with spit if they looked dirty. She had her own room down

THE COMMUNITY CONTAINED TWO KINDS OF SUBSTANCES: THE abundant (flour, salt, toothpaste, Bibles, freezer jam) and the pad-locked (cocoa, colored pencils, moisturizer). Accordingly, Dorf children were devout dualists. Abundant items lived in the Help Yourself room, monitored and replenished by Stores. The knowledge that one could help oneself rendered doing so unappealing; abundant items were not worth hoarding. Help Yourself also served as a purgatory for potential garbage. There was always the possibility that someone might want two dozen plastic coffee scoops, or half a chafing dish of sweating pear crumble. Most offerings appeared and were just as mysteriously disappeared within the day.

Padlocked items lived all over the Dorf: in Medical, the Steward's office, the Sewing Room, and, most temptingly, in Stores. Stores was a vault of commodity, every special thing at once: candy bars, colored cellophane, spices, and ribbons. In the community's rigid supply chain, married couples and families received provisions from Stores in initialed plastic baskets available for pickup in the Help Yourself room after noon on Saturdays. Rarely did men come for their family baskets; unlike wives and mothers, they could not instantly parse the contents, and could not be trusted to refrigerate perishables or stow the toiletries that would mortify their recipients if left in plain sight. There was never any excuse for a child to be in Stores.

On the locked door hung a wooden box with a slot in its lid. Here one deposited requests: benne seeds for brittle for a birthday treat, or an extra canister of coffee in anticipation of guests. A met hamburger for lunch. Ruth remembered him trying to fry a cucumber one family supper; she'd understood even then that he was deeply, magnetically pathetic.


Should children pray? Arrayed in concentric circles in the Meeting Hall, the Brotherhood argued this point, diverging on whether prayer killed or quickened reverence. Rote prayer forced sentiment that should never be forced, said Edmund Dampf. Tobias Schmidt concurred: prayer created a barrier between children and God. Johann Braun questioned whether grace could be freely chosen.

When later Ruth learned of the Virtues, she was surprised that unity was not among them. As Paul told the Corinthians to be of one mind and one thought, so did the Brotherhood hallow and chase and bait it with prayers. The elders enforced the law, but only complete, collective unanimity among baptized members could adjudicate it. Seeking unity was the spiritual corollary to the physical labor of chopping wood and canning produce. It was what caused weeknight Meetings to run on for three hours. Seeking unity wearied even Esther Scholl to permissiveness.

All were implicated by a deadlock, a form of shame that was itself unifying. From the back row, a feeble voice began "The Manx Fisherman's Evening Hymn," and almost everyone was glad to join in; after a few more songs, contrition and humility prevailed. The Brotherhood knelt and prayed.

Ruth could say the Lord's Prayer quickly but not slowly, and learned the Apostle's Creed as she learned cursive handwriting: in secret, by crude, misunderstanding mimicry.

them to get to God, but as they were commanded, they let the little children come and go freely.

RUTH'S MOTHER SPOKE TO HER IN HUTTERISCH AT HOME, AND consequently Ruth never learned whether the language had application beyond scolding. The soft Colony pidgin was full of words for dumplings, mucus, and foolishness. She knew that Hutterisch was not written, and assumed this to be a failure of the alphabet; decades later, on the internet, her queries would return phonemes so exotic that they appeared as empty rectangles on the screen.

Esther often accused Ruth of *buddling*, a singular sin from the Western Colonies. To *buddle* was to waste time on little jobs; to fuss, to fiddle, to sit in a corner skinning twigs with the edge of a spoon instead of tidying up.

Buddling connoted no mischief, only diversion. As with lactation, boys would not or could not buddle.

RUTH HAD NO INTEREST IN HUMAN BABIES AND REMEMBERED little of her baby sister's realization. She imagined only a mother-shaped balloon, slowly inflating with pudding and marrow. Sue Ellen was an early coda to what should have been a larger family, greedily sealing Esther's womb against further children.

Esther stayed in the hospital for two weeks after the birth. No one had yet been sent to help the family, so their father made do, serving drop biscuits every morning and butter sandwiches or plain song known to pacify lower creatures. When the eft's soft outline stopped twitching beneath the handkerchief, she prayed for it to stay alive and was relieved but not surprised by God's compliance.

Then Ruth had an idea so abrupt and precise that it had to be holy orders. She would send Olfetter and Ankele a present.

Her father found her an hour later behind the stables, sobbing and unable to explain why she had put a live eft into a bottle of dishwashing liquid. He was, as always, bewildered by her tears—immune to emotionalism but still powerless before it. So while she cried, he made an engineering project of extracting the softening carcass, which he then left in three pieces by the sink.

The Scholls had absorbed the trauma by suppertime, and Ruth was left to reflect privately and with deepening shame on her message from the angels.

FURTHER CONFUSING RUTH WAS A SECOND MYTHICAL PAIR OF ANcestors, Opa and Oma. Unlike her mother's parents, Opa and Oma were public knowledge. They led the community as a couple and were invoked in Brotherhood decisions, their health and guidance daily prayed for. If God protected them as often as He was asked to, Ruth's ambivalence couldn't do them any harm. She imagined them as anthropomorphized knife and spoon. She deduced that they lived overseas, perhaps in Europe or Germany, and that they shared responsibility for the Brotherhood with God Himself.

From beneath their purview, Ruth had no reason to fear Opa and Oma, so she didn't. Later, she would need to pass through able when her father became annoyed with her muttering and made her switch seats with James.

Ruth's grandparents were not in the photograph, and her mother would say only that they were named Olfetter and Ankele and came from the Western Colonies. Ruth imagined them sleeping under a rose petal in a walnut shell and leaping over candles. She told Dorothy Mueller, who at age five believed everything she was told, that she was related to Rumpelstiltskin.

THE SCHOLLS LIVED IN GRACEFIELD, ON THE FIRST KNUCKLE OF the index finger in the glove of Michigan; the most southerly of the Brotherhood's three North American Dorfs. Ruth recognized Gracefield as a complete ecosystem: it had forests, a lake, a library, a set of triplets, and her family. She, Jeremiah, and James often spent Sunday afternoon unsupervised in the woods behind the Laundry. Once, while her brothers were occupied pulverizing an especially brown rock, she went down to a pond where she had once seen a salamander and so now visited ritualistically. In a patient squat she stabbed the mud with a stick.

She was squinting to align two branches in the sunlight when something flickered in her peripheral vision. It was a red eft, and she covered it with one cupped hand just as Jeremiah and James crested the hill, come to daub her with rock paint.

The eft had the moist, crepey texture of an old person's hand, and glowed a toxic poppy. Ruth hid it under a damp handkerchief under an inverted canning jar while humming "Greensleeves," a provoked her inner imp. It scampered down to Hell and returned with sacks of obscenity: her parents dying, the private parts of cavemen and Egyptians in the children's encyclopedia, the words *shit* and *sex*. She hoped that those with access to her thoughts tuned in only occasionally, if alerted, and in that hope she was in ardent imitation of a child whose soul required no monitor.

Growing up, Ruth surmised, was the process by which one became opaque to God, and this was why nobody could read her mother's mind, or the elders'. Ruth thought of egg whites, clouding in a frying pan, and wondered whether she would still have evil thoughts when no one else could see them.

There was only one document of her mother's early life in the Western Colonies. It was displayed below the photograph of Esther's wedding day and above her brother Jeremiah's careful and menacing watercolor of the Virgin Mary clutching the baby Jesus. All three pictures hung behind her father's head on the wall that Ruth faced at the breakfast table. By closing one eye she could see through him, to the black-and-white portrait of seven grim Dettweilers posed beside a ditch, 1948.

The men looked like Abraham Lincoln. The women, even her mother, like rats in kerchiefs. Ruth had memorized the chevron and invoked them under her breath every morning before grace: Samuel, Paul, Simon, Else, Esther, Sharon, Rachel.

Her mother was thirteen years old in the photograph and seventeen when she fled east; the other six remained in black and white in South Dakota. Ruth knew that chanting their names would, by the power of prayer, make them aware of her, and she was inconsol-

She was named Ruth before anyone could intervene. Two days before Easter 1963, rising from his plate of Hamburg pie, her father asked the Brotherhood convened at Gracefield to welcome Ruth Della Scholl; without hesitation, they did. Later that night, Esther Scholl told her husband he'd chosen the ugliest biblical name she knew. It reminded her of nothing so much as a tuber.

"I would have called you Maybelline Raisinette," she told Ruth; one of her many benign conspiracies. Esther, illiterate until seventeen, hoarded words and deployed the best only in times of great suffering, or boredom.

Ruth cherished those two especially, but found neither in the dictionary when she was old enough to use it. Maybelline was likely a word to describe long hair—here a fantasied stallion tossed its head—and Raisinette an extinct form of credenza. This analysis she reported with solemn confidence to Dorothy Mueller, whose own enviable name meant gift from God.

GOD, JESUS, HER MOTHER, ALL OF HER DEAD RELATIVES IN HEAVEN: Ruth knew that each could read her mind, and knowing this only

# *Gracefield*

A small potato in the blight still strives toward the light.

BILL CALLAHAN, "DAY"

RIVERHEAD BOOKS
An imprint of Penguin Random House LLC
1745 Broadway, New York, NY 10019
penguinrandomhouse.com

Portions of this book were previously published, in different form,
in *n + 1* and *The Paris Review*.

Book design by Cassandra Garruzzo Mueller

Library of Congress record available at https://lccn.loc.gov/2024054781

ISBN 9780593715949 (hardcover)
ISBN 9780593715963 (ebook)

Printed in the United States of America
1st Printing

The authorized representative in the EU for product safety and compliance is
Penguin Random House Ireland, Morrison Chambers, 32 Nassau Street,
Dublin D02 YH68, Ireland, https://eu-contact.penguin.ie.

# RUTH

*Kate Riley*

RIVERHEAD BOOKS • New York • 2025

the hall but spent most of her time in the Scholl living room, her left leg extended on a gout stool, speaking to Esther in Hutterisch.

It was one of Ruth's more onerous chores to accompany Cynthia on Sunday afternoons to the orchard, where Cynthia practiced her golf swing on crabapples. Ruth thought her unfriendly for a woman with so few teeth. Moreover, she envied her Esther's attention.

Watching Cynthia work a slurry dough for pies, Ruth became possessed with the idea that she slept prostrate with a crabapple in her mouth, like a banquet pig from a storybook.

Up through kindergarten, children belonged to women, in whom both aptitude and intent to nurture were congenital. Women alone ran the Babyhouse, a pacific incubator which at nap times fell silent but for the gentle rustling of long skirts; men meant nothing to drowsy, heat-seeking infants. But scope for disobedience scaled with motor skills, and more than warmth was required to train and prune growing children. The Brotherhood concluded that, to replicate the harmonious marriage of love and discipline provided by a mother and father, every classroom in the schoolhouse ought have a male and a female teacher both.

Ruth, like Jeremiah two years before her, had Rupert and Fiona Wollmann for third grade. A couple in their middle years, of notable childlessness, they were the secret stars of every child's transfamilial fantasy: a life without siblings, where the clear, flattering light of Rupert and Fiona's attention was a permanent condition.

Each morning began with a song and a prayer, and ended with

three laps around the schoolhouse, Rupert galloping at the lead while Fiona wheeled the lunch cooler from the kitchen. After every noon, they commenced "Investigations," an improvised and legendary curriculum: James's class built a trebuchet, with which they launched overripe watermelons onto the shop roof, and in Ruth's year, Rupert and Fiona buried an abridged cow skeleton so that the third grade could discover, excavate, and correctly identify it as the Fartosaurus.

RUTH KNEW NO GREATER JOY THAN DISCOVERING A PRESENT AT her place at the breakfast table. Like all good and mysterious things, presents grew in the dark and appeared in the morning, evidence that the world conspired toward delight.

On her sixth birthday she woke before dawn and stood in the door of the living room, paralyzed with happiness at the silhouette of the items on the table. She got back in bed and prayed to God: If she went to Heaven, might she be six years old forever?

IN ADDITION TO BIRTHDAYS, CHRISTMAS AND EASTER TENTED the otherwise shapeless progression of seasons. The community could always be found waiting on one or the other. "Looking toward Easter" was a perfectly acceptable response to inquiries after one's activity.

Ruth was almost always looking toward Christmas, when autumn's ominous, perpetual dusk gave way to snowy mornings. The road to Heaven is Heaven and the road to Christmas, Christmas;

from the stollen of First Advent breakfast to the Christmas Eve midnight Meeting, she kept her mind to the Christchild.

The community provided a Douglas fir to every family on the Dorf, and with the trees came Ruth's favorite ritual: unpacking Christmas decorations. The deformed wax Santa and needlepoint snowflakes grew more magical in storage. She was prohibited from touching the crèche. It had traveled with her father's family from the Bavarian past and lived in a petrified nest of pink tissue paper. Its wooden stable was lined in real moss, the figures cast in plaster, and only Joseph much the worse for wear; he was appropriately helpless without hands.

Ruth visited the crèche reverently, compulsively. She was not so wicked as to ignore the cradle, but her true love was the dolorous, lamb-yoked shepherd boy.

For several hours, unbeknownst to itself, the community possessed Candyland. Ruth found three of its loosely associated cardboard quadrants in the milk crate of donated children's books, and confidently interpolated the fourth; though seized and destroyed before dinner, the game remained vivid to her for years. She drew her own wending maps of the Dorf, which was itself laid out like a board game requiring no skill: a single path along which all topographic features were decoration, not obstacle. One began at the Gracefield sign, mounted to a barrel-size concrete pillar upon which a succession of sisters failed to train ivy. The property had, before community acquisition, housed faculty for the nearby military academy, and its sterile barracks resisted domestication.

Ruth aspired to fidelity, and her maps always featured the aboveground septic cube as a discrete point of interest.

NEXT: THE SHOP, THE OFFICE, MEDICAL—IDENTICAL BUILDINGS that held nothing but busy adults. The small fleet of communal vehicles was parked behind Medical, and here Ruth drew a stretch limousine. Then the landscaped roundabout where they gathered in the relevant seasons; then the vast, vaulted Meeting Hall, with wings for the Kitchen and the Stores. There was a calculated rhetorical arc to the community's layout, one that Ruth traced at every subsequent Dorf: the Meeting Hall was its climax. The ceiling was higher than anybody could throw a rock and described an impossible geometry of intersecting posts and hammer beams. It smelled of cedar and beeswax. The Meeting Hall was as far as visitors ever came.

Thus were the Dorf's tenderest faculties hidden. Behind the Meeting Hall and obscured by a copse of maples stood the School, Laundry, and Babyhouse: buildings for women and children. It was in this fold that the Servant and his wife lived, cosseted among the precious. In Gracefield, Oma and Opa occupied the second floor of the Babyhouse, breathing milk-burp air.

This cloister would remain, even in Ruth's adult mind, the definition of home safe. These buildings were not inherited bunkers, but rather purpose-built by the community, half-timbered and green-shuttered in Bavarian style. Their resemblance to the house at the end of Candyland was incontrovertible.

Each floor of the dormitory itself had been renovated to the same plan, with space for two families, two married couples, and four singles (one for each household). The singles slept in a long corridor with curtains for walls, so narrow that they had to prop their cots sideways to dust mop. Married couples, who had earned privacy from others in exchange for nudity before each other, were provided a bedroom and a living room. Families were allotted an additional bedroom but were expected to make it stretch; a third bedroom was rarely granted before a fifth child.

Each floor shared a kitchenette, a cleaning closet, and two bathrooms, their communal use and maintenance a constant opportunity for sisters to sin. Domestic crimes—an oven light left blazing overnight, tidal scum in a bathtub—tempted women to furor the way women tempted men to lust.

The Brotherhood was enterprising in those years. They baked bread, brewed beer, and, to their own confusion, flew a chartered plane for the rare upstate businessman of means. Many ventures succeeded, and for two years Stores ordered name-brand ginger ale with which to stock the airplane cabin mini fridge. Didn't the Scriptures exhort them to be as clever as snakes? But all were uneasy with pure profit, and they thrilled at Hans Hauptmann's proposal to breed working dogs for both sale and donation. He quoted Genesis about man's duty to rule all the creeping things that creep; at last Ruth could claim a favorite verse of Scripture.

Kennels rose behind the wood lot, and from Germany came a pine crate containing a shepherd bitch named Schatzi. The whole community processed past her cage as though she would prove more than a dog; the third and fourth grades even sang her a traditional Tyrolean shepherding song, during which she reentered her crate.

Hans Hauptmann, excused from his regular accounting duties

to steward the breeding, spoke of the process in terms beyond comprehension, and thus beyond scandal. Thus did Schatzi acquire her first sire, Apollo, a handsome and hypnotically dim animal by whom she bore two litters. Of the first, only one puppy sold, and to a neighbor. Hans was confident that time would bolster their reputation, and meanwhile encouraged families to take liberally of the whelping box. Jeremiah and James chose Kipper, and Ruth's father staked him in the yard, where he keened and cried and nonchalantly defecated across his fourteen-foot radius.

Kipper was a yard dog for just three days before Esther lost patience and brought him into the house. He proved quieter in proximity, and, though an idiot like his father, pleased the Scholls tremendously. Many of his littermates were incompatible with life, while two were viable but bizarre; down the hall, the Knultzes had to muzzle their Prince to keep him from eating linoleum, while the one bought dog died at eight months, rumored to have lapped shoe polish.

Ruth loved Kipper and fed him everything she tired of. One evening, observing his optimistic circuit around the table, she realized he had an inner life and wondered at it. She asked her family whether Kipper knew he was a dog.

Her mother supposed so—"He sure doesn't think he's a rutabaga"—while her father understood the question.

"He doesn't know the difference between dogs and people," he offered, then paused again to watch Kipper watch the table. "But he understands that this is his family. He probably thinks that he's one of you."

Kipper thought he was a child, thought Ruth, just as she thought she was a child. How could either of them ever be sure? She knew of nothing true enough against which to test her hope. She watched Kipper in sad sympathy.

Schatzi's third and ultimate litter produced eight puppies. All could see that an anonymous and evidently petite sire had replaced Apollo. In time, Hans sought the Brotherhood's forgiveness and resumed accounting; Schatzi died upright at twelve years, her dysplastic hips cradled in a sling custom made by the Shop.

ON NEW YEAR'S EVE THE BROTHERHOOD GATHERED TO PRAY AND sing in anticipation of 1970. Ruth watched the procession of grown-ups tramp through the snow toward the Meeting Hall. She picked out her mother's pigeon step and her father's high Astrakhan hat; James and Jeremiah, just that year old enough to attend the Meeting, flanked their parents, no doubt feigning solemnity. The Deacon scanned for latecomers and bolted the cedar doors against the cold.

Ruth found Dorothy Mueller in the hallway their families shared. In nightgowns and snow boots they went down to the lake, whooping the one decipherable line of "Auld Lang Syne" over and over. Dorothy began chanting in a German accent that had tipped into Cockney by the end of the Lord's Prayer. It was a gaspingly dry night, and performing insanity inured them to the cold.

It grew later, and they louder. Neither heard when, in the new year, the Brotherhood reemerged from the Meeting Hall to joyful bed; nor did they notice when a hooked silhouette appeared at the top of the hill. It cleared its throat and they startled to attention. It was old Merlin Klee, shaking his head once and announcing, in a speaking voice, "That'll do."

As with baptism and marriage, dessert was not a given. One could expect it at Love Meals and Brotherhood Meetings, but otherwise only the kitchen's whims proved determinant; and though bowls of fruit were set out at the beginning of the meal, to be skinned and salted as accompaniment, proper dessert appeared—if it appeared—only after the entrée had exited.

No longer in a spell of involuntary poverty, the community had created a modest purse for proper sweets. Parsing the concept took several months and two Brotherhoods, as few trusted themselves to administrate indulgence. Lovers of licorice, dark chocolate, tapioca, and rice pudding all laid their preferences before the Cross in hope of peace and unity. They prayed through quorum to unanimity. Qualifying desserts, in order of rarity and appeal, were ice cream, chocolate pie, fruit pie, iced sheet cake, puddings and Bavarian creams, nude sheet cake, stewed fruit with dumplings, gelatin molds, muesli.

There was no plainer barometer of the kitchen's mood than muesli. In high spirits they garnished it with almond clusters, strawberry freezer jam, or even chocolate chips, while in resentment they had been known to offer only wet oats thatched with shredded apple.

"I'd rather have no dessert at all," Ruth announced upon excavation of one such offering.

Her mother regarded her with aberrant sternness. "You should be ashamed of yourself, Ruth."

And though she was, incurably, she rejected her mother's offer to change her mind.

"THERE MUST NEVER BE TALK, EITHER IN OPEN REMARKS OR IN insinuation, against a brother or a sister, against their individual characteristics—under no circumstances behind the person's back. Talking in one's own family is no exception."

The First Law of Roßdorf ruled on walls in homes and offices, hung in both barns, the stables, and at twenty-foot intervals in the hangar-length Shop. Typed and laminated, indistinguishable at a distance from building code boilerplate, the signage occurred more often than light switches. And it worked; the community spoke straight, in love, in obedience to a tiny sign of tenuous scriptural precedent.

Oma Anna's advice to weary brides was the only command as prevalent, though it remained in the oral tradition alone. The only solution for anger at your husband is to bake him a pie. Ruth heard it first from her own mother, and understood: daily acts of love were the best way to express anger.

Her mother was, by pure incidence, one of Oma Anna's twenty-nine nieces. Esther did not favor her aunt; at that volume all descendants ceased proprietary claim, and anyway family was a false God in a true Brotherhood. Ruth was taught to see that Anna was not merely Esther's relative but her sister, like every other female in sight.

Like Esther, Anna had wed in from the Western Colonies. She

was a consummate wife and home economist, blessed with virtues in both roles. Humility, patience, diligence, and temperance; thrift, jollity, wisdom, and contentment. They dwelt in her like the hollow in a tree. Anna was one of a passel sent east after the first unification, political good faith expressed in the age-old exchange of virgins. The subsequent stunts of marriage—five Stahl brothers from the Colonies wedding five of the Brotherhood's Hauptmann sisters on New Year's Day, most fruitfully—outlasted all shifts in alliance between the regions and produced some of the Brotherhood's most revered pairings.

Anna married William Ayler, a sobering brother, lanky but tilted from polio. They were the first couple to wear the Brotherhood's own wedding rings instead of the plain silver bands that voluntary poverty mandated; gold plate, incomplete circles open in the shape of the Cross, symbolizing (the words now vacant from repetition) the way of love open to all through Christ. Anna was the first to discover the inconvenience of an open ring on a laboring hand. Clever with a soldering iron, William ran a thin wire beneath the open Cross, symbolizing utility or perhaps just consideration for Anna.

Each of William and Anna's six children remained in the community, though all four girls remained single-hearted. William Junior, called Wilb, married young and hastened to make Anna an Oma. A midnight stroke took William just the year after, so it was given to Margrit, their youngest child, to remain at home and tend Anna into old age.

Anna was eighty-five in Ruth's first memories, mobile and vocal and, with Margrit, the Scholls' regular Tuesday supper guest. Ruth could not imagine Oma Anna crying, and yet did not fear her. Anna was simply full of grace.

EACH DORF HAD ITS OWN JURY OF ELDERS, PAIRS OF MARRIED couples upon whose hearts one was invited to lay all fears and desires; they, in turn, did their best to channel God's will into practical operations. As daily life was itself the sacrament, each decision elaborated the community's theology; every Dorf expenditure, every song expunged from the songbook, every courtship frustrated was the consequence of powerful prayer, and as such unquestionable.

Though one could, in theory, approach any elder with any matter, there were certain sympathies to ford, certain specialties of prayer: one couple reliably supportive of the young people's ambitions, for example, or elders who had themselves lost a child and so required no imagination to counsel grieving parents. The ban on submitting the same confession to multiple elders was tacit but absolute—they shared a brain, if not a heart. The most elderly elders of all were the Servant and his wife.

Though anticipation of Christ's coming never grew old, to wait for worldly change was to live preoccupied. The community acted without warning, sparing its members the anxiety of any fixed future; nothing was certain but that they could rejoice in the Lord, always. The elders spirited families from Dorf to Dorf with only a day's warning, the better to induce gratitude for a life without private property to pack.

No worldly algorithm predicted circulation among the Dorfs. Some families moved yearly, while others grew where they were planted.

RUTH HAD THE END OF ONE BRAID BETWEEN HER TEETH WHILE she finished the other, but released both as soon as Dorothy appeared in the corridor.

"We're not Christians," Ruth announced. "My dad said."

They shuffled in their socks to the shared supply closet opposite the Knultzes', dropping automatically into whisper; Karin Knultz, a middle-aged creature of villainously bad humor, lived to lurk and scold. The girls were meant to be filling buckets at the mop sink while their mothers swept; after breakfast and before school was their first, if not best, chance to clean the floor. Ruth lashed her braids together under her chin and blustered on.

"He said we use the word *Christian* like we won an award. It's stuck up."

Dorothy filled her bucket first while Ruth did sliding lunges across the threshold. Activities were under a half hour Dorf-wide delay as grace for a sleepless night. Vague Trautel Klein had passed into eternity in a protracted deflation that left her body a pancake under the blankets. The whole Dorf rotated through Trautel's bedroom until the early morning, when her eyes finally fixed on a vent in the ceiling and never closed.

Returning from their families' vigil shift, Dorothy had explained to Ruth that candles were made of dead bodies.

Now, bucket frothing with diluted Zep, Dorothy was the naïf. "What are we supposed to be called, then? Are we gentiles?"

Ruth, who did not know, quickly reproduced her father's claim that one should aim only to be a follower of Christ. "He said it's the difference between being a noun and a verb."

From down the corridor they heard the arrhythmic, orthotic footsteps of Dorli Braun, one of the last surviving sisters from the founding community. She trudged into view, unlit cheroot clamped and dampening in one corner of her mouth, and dipped her head in acknowledgment as she passed. She spoke no English.

Dorothy waited as Ruth crouched by the spigot. "What's the difference between a noun and a verb?"

That was easy. "A noun is a slow verb."


RUTH'S FATHER RAN STORES, A ROLE HE ACCEPTED IN HOLY OBE-dience and frustration. While other men labored with their hands, he sourced vats of discount mustard and attended institutional trade shows. Ruth didn't mind the fact or frequency of his absences from the Dorf, but she did suspect him of some vague and filthy betrayal every time he came home.

Who wouldn't struggle for purity in the stained Minoan halls of the Ramada? The plastic bedspreads and television channels horri-fied him; he came to impute vulgarity even to the off-white regula-tion plastic coffee carafes. The blankets. The particleboard drawers. Returning to Esther after these trips, he thought often of the purity rituals of the Old Testament.

He dreaded the convention mixers most, and to his family described the horror as comedy. Finger foods alarmed him; he was always indisposed, both hands cramped with wadded napkins, when the cocktail weenies finally circulated. Could the waitresses and his fellow attendees read his distress? He wanted to show them photos of his children, to explain that they sang before meals and shared all their possessions, as the Acts of the Apostles described. Scanning the crowd for other Christians struggling for the Kingdom, he saw only sunburned, suburban men, drunk in the afternoon, trying to trick one another out of money.

For three days he participated in the Midwest Industrial Kitchen Expo of 1969, held at Milwaukee's Comfort Inn. He stayed in the hotel, pained at paying thirty-five dollars of the Brotherhood's money each night for the indignity. He could not even repair to his room without shame, since ascent from the lobby, misty with chlorine and ferns, required taking either the slow glass elevator or the shallow curved staircase. He activated the fire alarm trying to access the utility stairs.

His room had been smoked in recently. He drew the curtains against the parking lot and put on the navy-green suit Esther had sewn for the occasion. It came from the same oddment as the house curtains; each evening he emptied the pockets of business cards and hung it tenderly in the empty closet. In his undershirt and underwear he slouched on the edge of the bed and waited for the words of the Gideon's Bible to strike him.

The fourth and final day, he and the suit attended a closing ceremony in the Annex Banquet Hall. He had failed to find anyone vending or even willing to vend Combotherm ovens in the US, and so onward he plodded among the booths, praying to be grateful, eager to be home.

He returned to the Dorf in his head, imagining how Esther had led the children into Family Meeting, perhaps encouraged the boys to join the next-door Wollmanns on their Sunday trek after lunch; she was helping Ruth embroider a performatively secret present for his birthday, and might have wanted the time off her feet moreover. He saw that it was gone three, the Family Meeting had ended hours before; he would be lucky to arrive before Esther slept. Forlorn and betrayed by a canapé, he suddenly and absolutely knew that he was under surveillance.

He found himself embraced, released, and then standing before a comprehensively freckled Black fellow in a pistachio-colored suit.

"Glory be to Jesus," said the man; at least he told the truth. Ruth's father held tomato juice in one hand and several spent toothpicks in the other, but could not keep this stranger from grasping his sleeve. Praying for courage, he caused himself to trust, and had within the hour placed an order for a hundred gallons of ice cream to be delivered on the first of each month from Frozee's Surplus Warehouse. Frozee's sounded a patently Godly enterprise; his pistachio acquaintance, Frozee president Lucien Dardenne, began every business day with a prayer to serve and honor however circumstance allowed, and attended church with several of his employees. Lucien too had despaired at the convention's spirit, and for one lapse into unchristian judgment both men spoke of the gathered salesmen as though they did not stand among them. Ruth's father, afraid to court vanity, did not ask what had marked him to Lucien as a follower of Christ, and Lucien did not volunteer that the combination of ungainly suit and suspenders had given him away.

The ice cream deal bore only fruit. Frozee's superior product and delirious pricing delighted the community, and Lucien visited the Dorf often before selling the company to a nephew and returning to Belize. Though ice cream was cheap, and easy on the kitchen sisters, and Frozee's variety sampler uniformly pastel-flavored, rationing kept it special. Stores provided a tub for every birthday child; otherwise, ice cream was reserved for historic anniversaries, sliced into inch-square cubes to facilitate fair meting. On such occasions, Ruth's father let his family serve themselves as conscience permitted, and was troubled by how predictably they responded to his experiment in scarcity.

For her eighth birthday Ruth received a sewing kit, a tassel of rainbow embroidery floss, a folding magnifying glass, a tin of Dutch process cocoa, and pajamas made of orange cotton calico into which her mother had already sewn a name tag. Jeremiah gave her a wooden duck with a clothespin for a beak, and James a sequence of nautical knots pinned to a card. She was allowed to wear her pajamas under her jumper to the morning Meeting, in which the announcement of her birthday occasioned both song and ceremony: three-year-old Marietta Becker, whose father led the Meeting, wended bashfully through the seats to deliver a candy bar tied to a helium balloon.

Ruth was clever enough to misunderstand all that she did not like. When her mother whispered to put the candy away, Ruth unwrapped and ate it; when, Meeting ended, Esther silently reboxed all of Ruth's presents and closed them in the high cupboard, Ruth condensed in fury. Instead of striking her mother, she slapped the floor, an impotent gesture that Esther ignored. "Don't show off," she said, and stepped over Ruth's possum body in the threshold.

RUTH KNEW SHE COULD NOT BE ENTIRELY DEFECTIVE, BECAUSE she loved Christmas. To have the trust of babies and animals; to delight in a God who made lady slippers and spotted toadstools; and to know with mind, body, and soul that God hung lower during the Christmas season: these were the qualifications required for humanity, and at least she managed one.

The Brotherhood lived in a constantly recalibrating state of voluntary poverty. Bouts of drastic rationing—two recent years when Stores abstained from ordering any seasoning but salt—were followed by longer phases of slow bloat. The fluctuation of luxury was only partly economic: anything the young people coveted was likely to prove too expensive to supply. Ruth wondered in which economic model one could identify poverty by the absence of baseball caps, highlighter pens, and nonmedicated skin lotion.

When word came that Sugar Valley, another Dorf, had shuttered its sauna as a measure of austerity, Ruth was perplexed. A category error, surely: the sauna was an essential facility, not an extravagance. Among exiles from the Colonies, there was firm consensus on the necessity of steam in daily life; as Cynthia explained, "It's the same as we cook the meat for, to kill the"—she turned to Esther—"*Winzige Würmer*?"

Esther finished her row of knitting before translating. "It kills the parasites."

"Worms," said Jeremiah, to himself.

And so Ruth had followed Esther to the women's sauna every Saturday afternoon as soon as she was old enough to tend a fire. She carefully piloted her child-size laundry cart (cargo: two towels, Esther's swimming costume, various deformed plastic measuring cups with which she pretended to cook) down the graveled path behind the Shop. While her mother changed, Ruth checked the furnace and determined what to feed it; the sauna had its own wood pile, presumably replenished by the same entity that set the fire every morning. (She knew, but did not dwell on, the popularity of this kind of furnace among Grimms' witches.)

Ruth wore her swimming costume under her clothes to avoid changing twice; standing on one foot, naked, in a wet tile stall with a curtain for a door, seemed to her at eight (and later, at fifty) the dumbest thing a person could do. She always beat Esther to the steam room and requisitioned the ladle.

They stayed and steamed for no more than twenty minutes, obviously the time it took to extinguish worms. Esther never looked more beautiful to Ruth than after the sauna: irregular arabesques of damp hair around her face, dilated eyes unfocused until she'd cooled enough to wear her glasses. As curative rituals went, the sauna was preferable to everything but purple Dimetapp.

No other Dorf prohibited sauna use, and Sugar Valley lifted the restriction after only a few months. Years later, Ruth learned that it was not austerity but temperance that the community had sought; Susie Dreiser, who had grown up there, confessed that her older brothers had been among those caught using the sauna for beer parties.

SUDDENLY, SEISMICALLY, THE WESTERN COLONIES ABSORBED THE Brotherhood. Unity with the West brought polka-dotted kerchiefs, black Sunday jackets, potato dumplings, and a cedar ark of historical sermons that emitted silverfish and had to be incinerated. Unity with the West robbed the Brotherhood of candles (accessories to fire worship), musical instruments (biblically unprecedented), and dolls (baals).

The doll ban was announced in a Brotherhood Meeting and enforced that same night. With doubt but in holy obedience, Esther confiscated Ruth's baby-doll and replaced it with a swatch of buttercup terry cloth, knotted in one corner. Ruth, in the morning, was not even puzzled, having read of changelings in the encyclopedia.

LEORA MAERZ WAS MAKING HERSELF SICK. ALL OF A SUDDEN SHE was hollow, her big lantern of a Maerz skull obvious beneath the skin and body flimsy below. By the time the community noticed, she weighed at ten years old what she had at six. Ruth, at nine, was infatuated.

Leora vanished from classes and communal meals, but Ruth located her with magical thinking. By orienting her chores windowward, she could see Leora and her older brother approaching the stables every morning, and returning before afternoon snack. For three weeks she tracked the mysterious routine; even from afar, Leora inspired in Ruth an addictive fear. Leora's illness was sinful.

Leora reappeared, back in flesh, on Easter morning at the communal breakfast. The morning's double wedding did not distract Ruth; through vows and love songs she remained trained on the Maerz family, searching Leora's face for lingering deviance. With weight she returned to bland childhood, and ate her lamb sausage dutifully.

THE MASS OF ALL RUTH KNEW WAS A DOT IN THE VOID. As the dot grew, so too did its perimeter with the void; every factual acquisition indicated a tranche of new unknowns, education the process of becoming a competent librarian of her own stupidity. The discovery, age five, that some people did not live in communities with all goods in common—that in fact for most, home was a locked building full of private property—begat questions still begetting questions at age thirteen. At five her only outsider had been the propane-truck driver, for whom she'd conjured a whole parallel Dorf, an image still requiring active extinction every time he made a delivery. His real life defied both fantasy and reason: without support from a Laundryhouse and Kitchen, how did he have time to do his job? Without Brothers and Sisters, from whom did he accept admonishment?

Ruth read everything she could, learning early that few adults would interrupt a child absorbed in the Bible; only Esther noticed its frequent appearance around bathtime. And she read at random, though some spinal defect in the Scholl's huge KJV favored Chronicles I and II. There was a narrow stripe of the New Testament she knew from inhabiting it, but everything else Ruth read was either tedious or unbelievable: legal bickering about who was allowed to bury figs near a special wall, pangrammatical lists of names, the talking donkey in Numbers, and the queen in Kings who got eaten by dogs.

It took Ruth trial and mortifying error to learn what of the Bible was now accurate only in metaphor. Ethiopians, Jews, and Greeks still existed; Pharisees, Samaritans, and Barbarians did not. Magi still existed, as Persians. Leprosy still existed, pharaohs did not. At Saracens, Moors, eunuchs, Ruth wondered. Not to mention all that the Bible didn't: China, India, America. Outer space. The library's encyclopedias, clear and sedative beside the Bible's cryptic thrills, still misled; Ruth lived for decades in an alternate reality containing Zanzibar and dipsomania.

No matter her source, the world beyond the Dorf was always mediated, by time and human error; if the Apostles couldn't agree on the nativity, Richie Mueller's account of a ball python at the 4-H conference begged skepticism. Of those whom Ruth had license to pester, her father had seen the most of the world. He was off the Dorf every week in his role as Steward, but so weary upon return that Ruth knew to curb her curiosity; eyes closed, in his undershirt after a six-hour drive, he wanted his family close but quiet. Esther, chattier, had only the drifting details of her childhood in the Colonies for reference, and when Ruth returned to this closed canon it was for comfort, not news.

Truth in volume, then: Ruth read every periodical admitted to the library. In search of the evidence of strangers, she skimmed the essays of anodyne encouragement and skipped entirely anything accompanied by illustration of flowers or cornucopia. Missionaries were reliably specific; in a report to the *Friends Journal*, a Quaker medic working in Liberia felt closer to God without the luxury of refrigeration, and on the single typed page that constituted the *Brethren Witness*, a pastor in Luzon alluded to Papist savagery, then (see other side) offered the recipe for Coconut Surprise. Ruth spent the rest of her life poised to declaim Papism for sheer pleasure at the phrase, though it was the Catholic publications she savored most. Their faith had hands and feet; their service was not tourism but permanent residence in the world Ruth could only read of. In *Commonweal* a Berrigan brother wrote from jail of the hopeful solidarity among his Black cellmates; Catholic Worker newspapers, their cheap ink faded by an afternoon of sunlight, described finding Christ among tramps on the breadline and exhorted readers to join Him.

Ruth knew the community said the same thing—anyone reading the New Testament out loud said the same thing—and were dutiful in concern for all those implicated in both beatitudes and the Civil Rights Act. While shielded from much else of the decade, Ruth spent her portion of the sixties vividly alert to the struggle for racial equality; there was more moral clarity in the parables of Rosa Parks and Ruby Bridges than in much directly attributed to Christ, and many a Meeting in which the orchestrating brother had merely to cue a recording of "How Long, Not Long" or "I Have a Dream."

In practical matters, however, the community prioritized service to their immediate neighbors, via highway cleanups and pies of breathtaking uniformity donated to the county's Harvest Festival. Consequently Ruth's few excursions off the Dorf were unpeopled by the strangers she felt most moved to serve. She had never met a

Black person, nor anyone exhibiting signs of poverty; whatever love she could render went only to those she already knew, far harder to love for already knowing them.

There was rationale for the community's insularity: nourishment of the inner church precluded a robust missionary program; able bodies were needed on the Dorf, on fire for Christ in prosecution of daily tedium; pouring impossible from an empty cup, etc. This provincialism was identified as such and condemned by Merlin Klee, who had been a Freedom Rider as well as a Catholic before joining the community. In Meetings, Merlin sat agitated with a folder of newspaper clippings in his lap, occasionally shedding bleak confetti. His calls to action were invariably muted by prayer.

Ruth coveted Merlin's experience and wished to signal her righteous alignment. She imagined confessing to him a germinal scheme consisting of a single image: the community's young people alighting in Detroit. She had seen a picture of the City-County Building, so in fantasy it was always there they alit, though she had no visual for the generalized solidarity she anticipated once out in the world among authentic suffering masses. In the community her faith was stifled— bore only the unappetizing fruit of janitorial work and singing—but on the single imaginable street of Detroit, on behalf of those who truly deserved it, she would gladly risk injury, arrest, and, in what she would later recognize as the acme of her arrogance, probably her life.

UNDER THE GUISE OF AN ENGLISH PROJECT, RUTH INVITED MERlin to the Scholl family supper, where a single question after the blessing elicited narration that lasted through dessert. The notebook in which she had planned to transcribe his life story remained blank beside her place mat; Merlin's memories seemed sequenced in escalating order of impact on his heart rate, an achronistic medley ranging from the tranquil (his World War II posting as a cooper at the Bremerton supply depot) to the indelibly sad (the breath control required to evade beatings from his blind father on their sugar beet farm).

It had never occurred to Ruth that Merlin had passed through childhood, or existed in any state other than the shambolic crankiness for which he was known, and even with the benefit of his testimony she struggled to conjure his younger selves. He recounted early CORE meetings ("before we whites had the good sense to step back and shut up"), his fractious but illuminating correspondence with a Dominican proponent of just-war theory, and the spitting crowds in Winnsboro; his rotation through the South was weeks after the beatings in Birmingham and Montgomery, and his dismay at its relative bloodlessness came as an epiphany.

"I said the right things, and I did the right things, and I thought I was being an instrument of God's will," he explained. Sue Ellen had folded napkin fans for each place setting, and Merlin now idly straightened the pleats on his. Though standard practice in family meals was for whichever children were capable to wash the dishes before dessert, Esther herself cleared the table so that Merlin could retain his audience.

"I wanted them to attack me so I could be a hero." He scanned the table, and for a moment Ruth froze in the crosshairs of his attention. "My activism was ego worship plain and simple. Community is the only cure for people like me."

At their table sat Merlin, cured; picketing Woolworth's, considering the priesthood, taking a pilot boat without permission to explore Puget Sound under a full moon: Did he renounce all these as sickness? How was she to cure her own ego if an entire lifetime in community hadn't? Her mother returned with Jewish apple cake, and Ruth abandoned composition of the clause-studded question she'd been planning all evening.

"Then why do you keep saying we should go out and protest and lay down our lives?"

Both of her parents stated her name in unison; after a pause, Merlin answered, tone unchanged.

"I'd be afraid of the world too, if I'd grown up here. But it's people like me, people who want to be heroes, who should stay out of the action, and people like you who can do it with a humble heart."

Ruth felt herself glow with anger as Merlin resumed his monologue. Her throat closed tight around the spiked horse chestnut of her voice box; she began dismantling her cake with the brutality of a combat surgeon, prizing out chunks of apple until only the pocked superstructure remained. The instant Esther repeated her name—volume lowered, reproach amplified—Ruth pushed away from the table and left the room with what she hoped was the air of one fulfilling her destiny.

The next morning she found her ravaged cake where she had left it, and, in boxy, unfamiliar print, "HAVE COURAGE" at the top of her notebook page. A classic diagnosis of a common deficiency; but it was relief from pride and curiosity that Ruth prayed for. As with all worldly ambitions, the desire was the disqualification, and the only way to get what she wanted was to stop wanting it. She wanted desperately to join the Longest Walk, to protest apartheid with students at Michigan State, to make her own small life rise like a welt in the raking light of history. Each intrusive fantasy of public heroism confirmed the futility of her prayer life.

It did not occur to Ruth until middle adulthood that her own anxiety about performing goodness might have been synecdoche, and that the community itself refrained from demonstrative virtue for fear of its own motives. So she remained a nervous island on a nervous island, unworthy of seeing and serving the world, limited to implication and the imagery of pamphlets. Black people, along with the poor and the unborn, were ever but only present in theory, elect in affliction and loved in abstract.

Though the Brotherhood regarded all forms of worldly authority with skepticism, they were as uneasy with Christian anarchists, whose ranks grew unchecked in the late sixties. ("That's what happens when the Catholic breeding program meets Vatican II," declared Merlin Klee, often and within earshot of children.) Nearly every weekend during the late sixties, unisex young people in dungarees had come to spectate life on the Dorf. Nearly all left with their righteousness intact. They faulted the Brotherhood for conformity: the costumes, the state and federal taxes rendered, the yearly contribution of Dorf-processed wurst and hamburger to the police community picnic.

The Brotherhood brooked these criticisms with polite equanimity, for all ignored the true spiritual crisis intrinsic to their way of life. It was worship of the family that tempted the Brotherhood;

who among them had not taken his eyes off the Cross to cast a protective gaze over his wife and children? How many mothers could mete love in identical portions and resist favoring those they'd borne? Family was all the more dangerous for being good and right—in each living room lurked a private tribe, declared one Servant, and repeated all others.

The community was more shocked by accusations of sexism. The synarchy of wives and mothers might be too subtle for outsiders to comprehend, but was marriage not a prerequisite for leadership? Didn't every Servant serve only by the grace of his wife, without whom he would be exhausted, hungry, and without family?

The Brotherhood prayed to break the spine of family worship. The elders convened. After three days in catered isolation, they returned to their respective Dorfs and announced a new category of person: the Shalom.

Now, instead of remaining with their own parents until marriage or orphanage, young people would be assigned to serve another family, and to rotate around the Dorf as practical and spiritual gaps demanded. This new way of life would provide the structure of kinship while precluding festering intimacy.

The Shalom would also have group activities to themselves, the elders forecast, interacting "freely and unselfconsciously" while hiking, completing work projects, and discussing serious issues in a weekly assembly. A snack budget had already been allocated.

All single people between the ages of sixteen and thirty-five were conscripted and rehomed within the week. Those over thirty-five—

an overwhelmingly female group, sisters who had, with varying concession to grief and bitterness, remained brides of Christ—were let be.

Each newborn Shalom person belonged to and depended on his or her host family as they had with their own. The group was immediately, in language and in life, subdivided into Shalom boys and Shalom girls. Duties were unchanged—Shalom girls still cooked, cleaned, and wiped little faces free of jam as they had at home; Shalom boys still helped wash dishes, but in the parallel universe of an alien family. To produce a pair of fried eggs for an adult male who was not your father became the private referent for every Shalom girl learning the word *unheimlich* in German class.

The elders made the Shalom, and saw that it was good: where intimacy once threatened, the young people were now safely suspended in a state of familiarity without favoritism.

THE INNER AND THE OUTER, AND WHETHER EITHER WOULD MATTER in Heaven—vehemently the community professed a Lord who heard their secret groans and saw through their human costumes. "Tomorrow we could all decide to wear bell-bottoms," said many people, many times, to illustrate just how little God minded appearance. Yet, year after year, they remained in costume, trying to grasp the eely virtue of modesty. And one by one, their staple garments disappeared from catalogs.

When their last remaining source for sanitary belts became insolvent, they bought up enough deadstock for a decade. Ruth was one of the group of Shalom sisters conscripted to divide and relabel the pallet for distribution among the Dorfs. They were nearly finished before anyone noticed that Ruth had written "Moths & Rust" across the top of each box she packed. She had used permanent marker, rendering the boxes unusable; the entire Shalom was invited to forgo their planned bonfire and meet with elders Ursula and Jörg to discuss the place of irreverence in the life of the church (nowhere).

Other items went extinct too quickly to stockpile. To compensate, the sewing sisters worked evenings to supply the community with homemade underwear in the traditional cut. The pattern was simple enough: stretchy bloomers that commenced at the navel and terminated mid-thigh, in a silhouette that Ruth understood in terms of Doric order (abacus, echinus, necking). Appropriating material proved harder: the sewing room's few bolts of jersey were intended for baby rompers and nursing hankies. Eventually, Stores was persuaded to order plain poly-blend tricot, but until then, any unmarried woman requesting new underwear got alphabet print or elephants.

It was a matter of protecting one another from desires. Men, not intrinsically beautiful, could show their boring bodies. But women had soft upper arms and bellies, bosoms, calves—none of which had anything to do with the selfless life in Christ. Assigned to clean the Babyhouse after breakfast with Susan Dettweiler, an older single sister prone to straight speaking, Ruth asked her why they had received this beauty only to hide it.

Susan was scouring a plastic potty, the last of ten. "Why did He make morning glories that go to heck as soon as I pick 'em?"

Even at fourteen, Ruth rolled her eyes at the old chestnut of omniscience.

"And," Susan added, "to make your husband feel special."

IT WOULD BE DECADES BEFORE THE COMMUNITY BUILT ITS OWN high schools. Until then, American law obliged participation in the public system, and so Ruth began ninth grade at Ogemaw Heights High School.

Ruth had imagined fast friendship with her classmates, whose ranks would include delegates from every chapter of the community's self-published modern American history textbook, *A Song for Many Voices*. She expected that within the semester they would be over at the Dorf after school, loafing in the grass under the bell tower, angling to stay for supper. The idleness proved fantastical: when they got back to the Dorf, Ruth and the other high school girls had ten minutes to deposit their book bags and change into work clothes before regrouping to give the Babyhouse its daily disinfection, after which came family chores, shower, supper. There was no time for school friends. Nor were there school friends.

The students from the Dorf coagulated defensively—there were fewer than fifty of them, marooned in a student population so big as to contain three separate girls named Lisa Miller, but little of the diversity Ruth had imagined, the only Black students two sons of a district court judge who transferred in her sophomore year. A sympathetic registrar was careful to align their class schedules, having learned from experience: When the community was new to the county, the initial group of students sent forth had no such protection, and, once dispersed, invited cruelties novel even to the guidance counselor. Two Ogemaw sophomores had barricaded a boy into a bathroom stall, his release conditional on identifying the Dorf sluts; girls were pinched, groped, and passed notes that made them cry noiselessly in the middle of class. Now, the community's youth were never without reinforcement.

In the cafeteria they ate in silence, consolidated their empty trays and silverware for the older boys to bus, and did homework until lunch was over. In a recent feint at austerity, the community had switched to margarine, and Ruth was among those who began taking extra foil-wrapped pats of butter home from school. The discovery of their theft precipitated one of the weepier group repentance sessions of her youth.

As students from the Dorf were categorically excused from P. E. (due to conflicting sumptuary laws), they used the period for self-directed and generally janitorial community service around the school grounds. The spring of Ruth's sophomore year, in a grievous misreading of the American teenager, they painted a mural honoring worker solidarity along one side of the gymnasium; Cesar Chavez's face loomed over the tennis court, gigantic and mild.

On the one hand, Christ was made flesh, and the body redeemed. On the other hand, young people had to be protected from themselves. Could sports be holy? Competitive games encouraged egotism when they were not an outright metaphor for warfare. The brothers' weight-lifting club was quickly and quietly aborted for fear of body worship. A young Zionist communitarian visited Gracefield. His more provocative details circulated rapidly: he was a vegetarian, drank tea and coffee mixed together, and would, when challenged, wearily explain why no Jew could profess pacifism. Ruth observed that he was perpetually humid-skinned, as though in his own private climate. The evening before he flew back to Israel, he taught the community a circle dance. Holding hands in a wobbling oval around the Meeting Hall bell tower, they danced to songs called (as he translated them) "The Fox Hunter," "The Gypsy's Earring," and "Grapevine of Zion."

They danced athletically, well into the night, with the older and younger among them occasionally breaking away to watch from the side. Ruth's parents were tireless. Her father leapt like a demon and wore the expression of someone performing complex aerophysical calculations. Esther was laughing and pendulous, meaty calves grapevining easily, bosom bouncing.

The circle dance trend swept the Brotherhood: first Gracefield, then Wheathaven and Sugar Valley. It became the default activity after Love Meals. Each community favored a certain version. Edendale specialized in the Fox Hunter dance, which required clapping hands beneath a high kick. There followed concern among the elders that some of the younger brothers were becoming vain and overly ambitious in their kicks, but in the end it did not warrant admonishment.

With lessening unease at the elision, Ruth learned to tell outsiders that the Brotherhood was part of the peace church, "like the Amish and the Shakers." This affiliation with the quaint and the stoic seemed to distract cynics and spared her having to explain their true order in the Christian taxonomy.

Like everyone raised in the community, Ruth knew the Reformation blow for blow; in fifth grade, her class had stormed the

Meeting Hall and nailed the Ninety-Five Theses to a preapproved door, using a real hammer borrowed from the Shop. Outside the community, had she trusted her inquisitors to listen, Ruth would have explained that Anabaptists believe that a true believer's baptism invalidates the dipping rite of infancy, and have believed it to the point of near extinction. Stateless and churchless, they had been chased across the forested margins of Europe, and martyred whenever caught. In North America, the survivors established church communities in which the Sermon on the Mount was their only charter, all goods were held in common, and a young person such as herself had no task higher than discerning whether to accept Christ into her heart and seek baptism.

Instead Ruth explained that, although the Brotherhood kept horses for recreational pony-cart rides, they were allowed to use cars.

THE LAMBING PROGRAM HAD BEEN INTRODUCED TO EMANCIPATE the Brotherhood from bought meat, with the ancillary spiritual benefit of domesticating the high school boys. As freshmen each received a gravid ewe and permission to miss school for delivery; while the inevitable stillbirth left its corresponding boy wrecked and ripe for Christ, by slaughter time, a month from Easter, it was hoped that every one of them had reread the story of the binding of Isaac. Four years in, most seniors found Isaiah 53 better consolation. In a community without private property, there was little opportunity for inheritance outside of genes and chores. Ruth was assigned the care of James's lamb the very day that he left.

As a freshman, Jeremiah was busy with his own flock of two, so

Ruth walked with him to the pasture beyond the wood lot every evening while Sue Ellen helped Esther clean the kitchen. Jeremiah's lambs, Mack and Jeep, knew their master's voice if not their own names, and always gamboled over to nibble at his ankles, but Ruth could not summon James's lamb, and even with pockets full of clover found herself the pursuer.

UNTIL NINTH GRADE, RUTH HAD HAD NO CAUSE TO DISTINGUISH the concepts of clothing and uniform. Everyone chose from their same few garments, every day, and ironing was the only possible gesture of formality. The community made no exception for its high school students.

For her first day at Ogemaw Heights, Ruth wore the best of her three skirts, a forest-green polyester that her mother had recently let out for the second and final time. She was relieved to see that the other girls from the Dorf were also wearing their favorites—anyone lucky enough to have a floral would show it off today—and imagined the impression they would make, gliding two or three abreast between classes, books held with casual modesty to their chests. They would appear serene and mysterious.

Theirs was the first stop on the school bus route; Ruth and Lotte claimed one of the prized wheel well seats and traded baseless speculation on the utility of learning French over Spanish. The bus doors had barely wheezed shut when, all around them, the boys started stripping off their chambray button-downs, showing their undershirts. By the time they reached the next stop, even the freshmen had quit their chambrays, and were indistinguishable from the boarding locals.

Assimilation was impossible for the girls. The garments Ruth witnessed in public high school achieved such intricate illogic that, even provided the resources and permission to waste them, she could not have sewn a plausible costume. On that first day alone, she saw: a mohair sweater with short sleeves; a sleeveless turtleneck; an alarmingly brief denim dress with suspender straps; a skirt made out of leather. Enumerating the varieties of blue jeans made her think very seriously of infinity. On the bus ride home, Lotte responded to Ruth's fashion observations with a steady blankness—community shorthand for: You are foolish and I am tired.

But Ruth could not stop noticing. The running list of exotic clothing she'd witnessed, sketched when words failed, ennobled her impulse to stare. At home she gave regular reports to Sue Ellen, and together they drafted a fashion pamphlet, sketching side by side on Sue Ellen's bottom bunk every night after supper.

Their pamphlet was completed in a single week and consisted of five original outfits and an accessories supplement that taught Ruth she could draw only left-facing shoes. The outfits kept well within the community's explicit parameters—only skirts and dresses, modestly obscure—but flouted every rule that could not be articulated. Sue Ellen drew a dress whose long, connected sleeves formed a jump rope; Ruth a floor-length gingham circle skirt with a place mat and cutlery pockets built in for picnics. There were fringe projectiles and hash marks of structurally redundant lacing, transparent rain boots ("see-thru" and an arrow pointing at an outline), and a purse shaped like a pastry bag. The outfits were modeled by head-less, handless figures whose necks flared oddly at the top; Sue Ellen rapidly surpassed Ruth in anatomical realism, for while they were equally inexperienced in figure drawing, Sue Ellen had not yet brooked the inhibitions that turned all of Ruth's bodies into sexless cartoons. Sue Ellen's outfits could, with imagination, appear to house the vaguest undulations of the female torso.

They presented the pamphlet first to Esther. "You'll not be wearing any of that," she eventually clucked, after skimming it at the breakfast table. She had not bothered to put on her reading glasses.

Undeterred, Ruth took the pamphlet to school two days in a row, but twice failed to plot the scene that would lead to her class-mates discovering it and expressing admiring wonder at her crea-tion. She thought about leaving it with the periodicals in the library, but did not want to part with her only copy. Sue Ellen's custody re-quest the following morning spared a third day of thwarted debut.

It was suppertime before Ruth saw Sue Ellen again, and without a word between them she perceived disaster. She did not ask what had happened—humiliation was deepest in the details—but in-stead attended to her heap of casserole with defensive gusto. Pre-sumably the project had been confiscated. She knew there would be no second issue. Worse, she knew that the elders, having found something worth punishing in its pages, would continue to seek and find it in whatever she did.

On the bus the next morning, the boys performed their now-routine removal of the chambrays. As they approached the second stop, Ruth interrupted Lotte's recitation of her French homework: "*Vingt-huit, vingt-neuf—*"

"I can't believe I used to care about fashion," she said, sounding not at all incredulous. "What a waste of time."

Lotte scanned the boarding group for offense. Most were in jeans and T-shirts, sweatshirts, baseball jackets. Only one girl wore a dress: long-sleeved, ankle-length, peasant-style, and printed to look like a patchwork of ditsy prints in romantic colors like eggplant and maroon. Lotte actually found it quite becoming, and said so. Ruth did too, but would not.

IN CLASS, RUTH DUTIFULLY PERPETUATED THE COMMUNITY'S REP-utation for generic excellence. She suspected that teachers had long since stopped bothering to read anything written in the community hand (a regular, robust cursive, even from the boys); at every essay assignment she considered and conquered the desire to fill the pages between introduction and conclusion with insipid synopses of her dreams. She accumulated useless AP credits knowing she would only ever be placed back in the Dorf.

Graduation occurred in paperwork that Ruth never saw. The community and its students never attended the ceremony, for several reasons: it glorified personal achievement; it took too long; their policy of abstaining from applause was glaring and misunderstood. Instead, the seniors were celebrated with a modest Love Meal, immediately after which they became Shalom. Now, instead of trailing their parents home in the evenings, they stayed on in the Meeting Hall with the incumbent Shalom. The boys moved dining tables and chairs to the periphery of the room, while the girls swarmed the kitchen to make Russian tea and slice a sheet cake into rectangles.

The boys set up the A/V cart, the girls guided two trolleys of snacks into the Hall, and then, on a flawless June evening, Ruth began her adult life in joyful rehearsal of an intricate mazurka.

MEN WHO JOINED THE BROTHERHOOD FROM THE WESTERN COL- onies were uniformly handy, gangly, and mute. They migrated in three clans: the Dettweilers from the Dakotas, the Wollmanns from Manitoba, and the Stahls from badlands across North America.

Among quiet men, Daryl Stahl was exceptionally quiet, and it was only by his oddly cultivated sideburns—long, but just shy of defiant—that he expressed anything that could be taken for personality. Daryl was sixteen when his family joined the community, and he, like all minors incoming, was borne on the faith of his parents. Whether he himself had felt called to leave Kilby Butte was irrelevant. To ask would merely reveal that spiritual Brotherhood could be weighed against elk hunting and found lacking.

Though obedient in his work, Daryl had managed to radiate unvarying joylessness in the two years since arriving. He worked with his father, Jedediah, in the production garden, and was mostly a silhouette plodding out to the orchard at dawn.

Esther Scholl was consequently perplexed to find a plate of cookies left on their kitchen counter: "With love, from Daryl Stahl."

Later that week, Lotte Schmidt received in her mailbox a careful illustration of two snowdrops, attributed to the same looping hand. She kept it in her Bible for two days and many prayers before showing it to her mother.

ONE DAY RUTH WAS SUMMONED FROM TYPING CLASS: THE SER-
vant's wife, Gerda, wanted to take a walk with her. They were out
past the stables before Gerda spoke.

"When we ask for baptism, we commit to complete honesty before God, and in the community that means complete honesty before our brothers and sisters."

Ruth watched her own feet kicking through wet leaves.

"I remember when I first requested baptism, I met with Oma
Annemarie to share my heart with her. And I shared the things I
wanted, and was afraid of, but I didn't tell her everything. And it
burdened my heart so much to keep things from her. So even after
we'd spoken for hours and hours, I wrote her a little note to say the
things I'd been too ashamed to say out loud. Just a little note in her
mailbox."

Ruth could not identify the string that Gerda was dangling in
her face.

"But I can't tell you how freeing it was to share my secrets with
her, and I went into baptism group feeling light and unburdened.
Do you understand what I'm getting at?"

Ruth snorted forcefully before remembering she had a rag in her
sweater pocket.

"I told Oma Annemarie that I was struggling with attraction. I
fantasized about getting married, and I was ashamed that I was
seeking baptism because of my own selfish desires."

Ruth nodded and, when Gerda gave her an imploring look, blew her nose. They walked on silently. Ruth touch-typed the alphabet in her pockets.

Gerda persisted. "It's only natural to struggle with attractions. But when we let our secrets fester, they lead to real sinfulness."

By the time they crossed Farrow's Bridge, Gerda's impatience was audible. "You need to put Daryl out of your mind if you expect Christ to find any place there. And not just for baptism. If Christ isn't at the center of your life, you can't even begin to think about membership or marriage here."

They were almost back at the Dorf, and Ruth could hear the snack bell ringing in the Meeting Hall. Without looking up she said, "I just thought it would be funny to pretend that Daryl—I don't know. I'm not attracted to him though."

Gerda watched her closely, then nodded and turned up the hill to the Redwood House. Defiance and sin Gerda could punish; defiance and sin could be healed. She knew no balm for oddness.

THOUGH RELIGIOUS SPEECH WAS KNOWN TO HIDE SNAKES, RUTH found even plain speech treacherous. She heard lies in every word, especially if she was the one saying them. Even confirming fine weather was a chance to sin. When confronted with a topic on which she had no thoughts, Ruth peeled into two, invisibly, and let her second self respond with pleasant vacuity while her true brain idled.

Salvation had come at sixteen years old in the discovery of the word *remarkable*: a self-fulfilling response to anything at all. The kitchen's attempt at Hawaiian pizza? The Gospel according to

Luke? A toddler on a leash in the aquarium lobby? Ruth remarked, and made them such.

FATHER VASILY, A FRAGRANT, EMBROIDERED DELEGATE FROM THE Eastern Rites church in Lansing, could not have anticipated the mania his Pisanki eggs would inspire. He laid a box of them while visiting for a 1979 conference on true Christian marriage, and returned the next year (colloquium on discipleship) to a community possessed. Pisanki eggs adorned houseplants and pencil tops. They nestled among cut flowers and wobbled in mobiles. As in the Passover story, with its blood on the doorframe, the presence of a Pisanki egg in a doorframe indicated that the household included a young woman.

The piety of decorative tedium was not disputed. The Shalom could not gather without the byproduct of craft.

Commercial dye was a rationed commodity, but two Dettweiler girls applied their Colony wits to synthesizing substitutes that produced a dull and narrow spectrum of beet reds. From the limited palette and absence of examples, radical schools of decoration arose. The term *Pisanki* came to refer to any egg hollowed, dyed, and kept out of reach.

The Shalom favored technically challenging samplers of Celtic knots and crosses, while the high school girls specialized in Navajo patterns. Some of the juniors, inspired by a research project on the Underground Railroad, attempted to re-create the slave quilt narratives in miniature and on eggs. The results caused great alarm at the Black Baptist church to which they were sent.

Ruth partook of the trend briefly, producing three eggs before a highly public retirement. The first two were portraits of Snoopy and Santa Claus, and the last was a birthday present on which she managed to misspell her own mother's name.

A community-wide hatred of omelets rose in correspondence with the mania for Pisanki eggs.

RUTH READ AT LEAST SEVERAL PAGES OF EACH BOOK ON THE REC-ommended shelf in Gracefield's library. Thus did she learn about the White Rose movement and apartheid and the child saints of Communist China, martyred in the Boxer Rebellion. Their martyrdom bothered her only by logical necessity, but the thought that many had come to Christ through divine inspiration—that miles from Bibles and churches, the person of Christ had appeared before these Chinese people, provided His name, and instructed them how to die in it—convinced her for several hours that she was not a true Christian.

Tolstoy's short stories were much loved in the Brotherhood; his mud imps and fighting bears occupied the same moral forest as Hansel, Gretel, and Baba Yaga. Ruth confused him with the English king who went mad and peed blue, as they both wore long white nightshirts in her mind's eye.

Wanting to be the sort of person who preferred *War and Peace* to *Anna Karenina*, she read half of the first and none of the second. It was just boring, she concluded privately. Nonetheless, the book retained pride of place on her nightstand for weeks after she'd given up on it, and whenever Tolstoy was mentioned she was known to observe that, for a follower of Christ, he seemed to care awfully about the downy upper lips of Russian princesses.

THE SHALOM WERE ENCOURAGED TO BE FREE WITH ONE ANOTHER at Singles Breakfast every Wednesday and Friday. The sisters arrived at six and, in the dimmed central kitchen, counted place settings, unpotted yogurt, brewed coffee and tea, sliced bread, and arranged six jars of jam to maximize diversity over three tables dragged in from the dining room.

Such low light in early mornings felt reverent. Even Ruth did not play the goat. Around six thirty, one brother, on a rota known only to brothers, appeared and made eggs in their midst. Who taught them to make eggs? How had Ruth's own brothers learned? Suddenly they were men, and she could not remember having ever understood them.

By seven, all who'd be there were there, and the egg brother would read something challenging and bless the meal. Conversation between brothers and sisters, when it occurred, tended to address the intractable calamities of breakfast service: the teapot spout that leaked if not greased; jam miscegenation.

AFTER BREAKFAST CLEANUP AND BEFORE WORK HUNG AN HOUR called Start, devised to keep everyone else busy while parents readied their children. Start was the time to do tasks like gathering eggs from the coop or updating the bulletin board with news of births on other Dorfs, or to buddle. Ruth's Start task was assigned in charity to her: she was to sit balanced on the radiator by Kathe Braun's bed and read children's stories to the elderly sister.

Kathe, for decades the community's only kindergarten teacher, never married, had been felled by a pair of strokes, and was now bedridden. Her face sunk and jutted, eyes closed and gray hair loosed from her kerchief, Ruth imagined her an old Native American man stoically mourning the land.

They began with *The Bronze Bow*, aimed at readers ten to twelve, an implausible sidebar to the Gospels in which a peasant boy met Christ. The author gave each character one adjective, and allowed each to keep it for the duration of the book. Christ, audaciously, was always and merely "kind."

Ruth loved to read out loud. She skimmed well ahead and anticipated the dips and slopes of intonation; she dismounted paragraphs with grace and admired herself for it.

Kathe was unresponsive and often asleep. The strokes had taken most of her voice and all of her English. She spoke rarely, and then only to decline Ruth's offers to keep reading. Eyes opened to lizard slits, Kathe would watch her for a moment and then wheeze a dismissive *nein*.

At 5:50 every Wednesday morning, fathers and sometimes little boys were sent to the central kitchen to pick up bread for the breakfast toast.

For the three weeks that Rhiannon Scholl did nights with Kathe and early mornings in the kitchen, the community suffered mushroom bread. Fathers sent for loaves often arrived in the kitchen before the bread did, returning late to their wives with steamed-up plastic bags and Rhiannon's deepest, sleep-deprived apologies. The bread, still half putty, would squash flat when sliced, but what could be done? Work started at 7:30.

Thus did the Shalom enjoy a rare unselfconscious moment as brothers and sisters, pretending to play accordion with Rhiannon's squashed bread at Singles Breakfast. Ruth looked down the table and saw the people for whom she would die. She loved them from deep inside her mind.

Suddenly she heard the tenor of performance in the breakfast hum. She identified the actors: Calvin Winslow and his roommate, Benji Blocher, a bull-shouldered teenager descended from one of the Brotherhood's great martyrs. Benji had just claimed that *Anna Karenina* was the best book he had ever read. Calvin glanced at Ruth for a second and then disagreed: *Anna Karenina* was, of course, a masterpiece, probably, but *The Brothers Karamazov* had challenged him in his faith. Steve Pfluger nodded with a mouth full of coffee. Ruth kept staring at Calvin.

The second time she caught his glance, she resolved to love him completely.

Rhiannon requested the Brotherhood's forgiveness.

Ruth next loved Calvin teaching trombone to four middle schoolers, every Sunday afternoon in the practice room off the dining hall. She could see him through the open door on her way to the kitchen, and so went to the kitchen compulsively, pointlessly, three times an hour until her mother insisted they go to the sauna.

For reasons obscure even to the brothers who made them, eggs at Singles Breakfast always arrived on a dinner plate covered by an inverted dinner plate, and were consequently warm but wet. "My eggs have perspired," Ruth said to Amy, and then looked quickly at Calvin to see him blush.

SHE FELT ONTO SOMETHING. HER EVERY THOUGHT AND ACTION was dignified by the prospect of sharing it with him.

On the Dorf, she located herself in relation to him. Calvin worked mornings on the Shop floor, a location where she could plausibly appear up to twice a week; the trick was then to get as close as possible while avoiding eye contact. He came in early and left late, and worked alone through Shop Snack in a T-shirt and protective gloves. She watched him from the catwalk and loved how stupid he looked. She was nauseated with affection.

Austeiler duty rotated daily, but favored the high school and Shalom boys, who brought a focused athleticism to their table service. They coordinated wardrobe, and for Love Meals wore slacks and button-downs over heavy work boots. At each meal, one brother distributed fresh bread wearing a single white cotton glove. Ruth became an astronomer and a particle physicist when Calvin was Austeiling, predicting his orbit as he served and willing him to obey her gravity.

In thrall, she requested baptism.

RUTH JOINED THE GROUP OF YOUNG PEOPLE WHO MET DAILY TO discuss baptism with the elders. She read the assigned Scripture and prayed for faith that would make her like a child, like a sheep, like salt: she prayed for faith, knowing it meant devolution. And yet every day she failed the same question with escalating intricacy. What was her relationship with Christ?

She babbled about salvation on the first day. Elder Ursula interrupted: Jesus Christ, the man. What was her relationship with Him? Ruth did not know, willed the world to combust around her, grew frustrated and then quiet. Kurt Ayler, archenemy of passion, provided the satisfactory answer while Ruth raged mute.

Ursula challenged her again the next day. Ruth would not lie: she had not met the Nazarene Jesus Christ. She had wondered and sobbed at the hope of redemption through suffering, and she had used His name to avow that hope, but no man walked beside her or comforted her in despair. How could any man be as real or true as the idea of Him?

All of this she had rehearsed on a loop since waking, and its deliverance was a relief. But from Ursula's radiating disappointment Ruth deduced that this, too, was the wrong answer.

On Wednesday the baptism group assembled before dawn to hike and witness to sunrise. The group—five young women and Kurt—met under the Meeting Hall bell tower and nodded greetings; the silence of the sleeping Dorf was as powerful as its noise in song. Elders Jörg and Ursula arrived last, she in child's hiking boots.

A single file, they entered the forest. Jörg carried a lantern, and

the trail flashed on and off with his lurching. Ruth, at the back of
the pack to better ford the shallows, tried to keep her mind in
prayer: she prayed God rid her of arrogance and fill her with peace.
She prayed that His will was for her baptism and that His will be
done. She forced her mind to Christ. She tried to stop thinking
about Calvin, sleeping baptized back on the Dorf.

Ursula was suddenly beside her, nimble on the dark path, invit-
ing confession with her silence. Ruth remembered her walk with
Gerda and surged with shame and defiance; she owed these little
old elves nothing. Nothing was louder than the kerchief muffling
her ears.

She turned her mind down and prayed to be a vessel.

"Oma, what is your relationship with Christ?" Ruth knew at
least this much of the script.

Ursula responded in the same childlike confidence with which
she plucked along in the dark. Her answer contained all the con-
stituent parts of a sentence but Ruth could not find any information
in it. That was what a relationship with Jesus Christ was like: beyond Ruth, too real and true for her own mind to hold; a man she
could know only from the certain pain caused by His absence. She
was tired and frustrated and began to cry just as they emerged on
Indian Head. Ursula grinned wide enough to show bridgework and
reached up to hug the finally dumb and humbled Ruth.

At Indian Head they formed a circle in the clearing and read
from John as the sun rose. Everything was edged in light; Ruth
was nearly beyond coping at how beautiful the world had become.
God was the trees and the sky and the line where they met, and that

she was allowed to see them at all. Remember to remember to re-member, she commanded herself. Grace was only the chance to see clearly.

It was in scouring Acts for practical guidance in living as the early Christians did that the Brotherhood had resolved to begin practicing the Eucharist in earnest. Thus had the Love Meal been instituted, and with it a dining rubric more arbitrary and baroque than the Hebrew Bible.

Love Meals designated special occasions: holy days, weddings, the arrival or departure of souls. Engagements warranted Love Meals, unless the wedding was to occur that same day; in such an event, a fancy snack and liquor at the engagement announcement would precede a full Love Meal after the wedding. Inter-Dorf Servant visits warranted Love Meals; so too tenth, twentieth, and all subsequent wedding anniversaries. Anyone nearing eternity was given a Love Meal, and as the Catholics practiced last rites so did the Brotherhood provide its dying with smoked meats and filter coffee after dessert. "And when the supper was ended," Ruth said as the Austeilers poured forth, carafes at a safe waist height. "Biblical schmiblical."

Love Meal menus varied with the preferences of those loved. Eugene and Yoona Park were confused although ultimately delighted by the kitchen's bibimbap endeavor. For Cornelius Braun's eighty-fifth, the entire meal was white, in reference to an anecdote everyone assumed someone else could make sense of.

Ruth observed that no matter the occasion and whatever else was served, a Love Meal was defined by the token sweet presented on a paper napkin. She withheld her finding from the community, well aware that every observation entered her mind a question and exited her mouth an indictment.

RECORDED MUSIC REMAINED CONTROVERSIAL ON THE DORF. It had been banned entirely under the yoke of the Western Colonies (for lacking scriptural precedent—but neither did beets appear in the Bible, groused Ruth, bothering the meniscus of her borscht), and the Brotherhood had only recently readmitted the possibility of music from a machine. From the county library's annual sale, Stores procured a box set of Beethoven symphonies performed by the improbable and audibly pastoral Kankakee Orchestra; here began and ended the community's record collection. Only Ross Becker ever listened to it on purpose, signing his name over and over in the lending library log; every Sunday afternoon he submitted himself to one symphony, and every Monday morning he announced to the Shop brothers that he had heard his favorite one yet. But Ross Becker was a man who rejoiced by default.

While the life of poverty protected most from their own desires, the community could never fully proof itself against a luring culture. Popular folk music riveted the Shalom; first transmitted by the collegers, Rosalie Sorrels's "Travelin' Lady" soon swept the whole younger Dorf.

Trend-weary, the elders banned singing any song outside the community canon. A brief humming epidemic followed. Could humming conduct sin? The ban was lifted in confusion. The Shalom were emboldened.

They requested a radio (not given), permission to attend a folk conference in Detroit (not given), permission to host their own folk festival (not given), and finally, taking the door that had gaped from the start, permission to perform for the community at Saturday supper (given).

The elders challenged Kurt Ayler to lead the evening. Such challenges proved hard to parse; even those chosen to conduct God's japes were not always quite sure why. Some Shalom were challenged because they were ready to be challenged, others because they were not. Kurt was built honorable: a cedar barn of a young man with no cause or capacity for deception. All saw the challenge as the first step toward Kurt becoming an elder himself.

Kurt set his plain mind to serving the community through song. Thus did he come into his Highwaymen albums: he wrote to the record label and asked for one. Moved by his lack of worldly property, the label sent back three LPs and a photograph of the band, signatures mimeographed. Per community rules, none of these gifts ever really belonged to Kurt, but it was still with some embarrassment that he surrendered the glossy photograph to the Steward. He was implicated by the vanity of those handsome men.

SATURDAY AFTERNOONS WERE RESERVED FOR WORK PROJECTS, during which young people were to interact unselfconsciously, getting to know one another by serving the community as brothers and sisters in Christ. Usually this meant landscaping. They dug ditches and planted fence posts and, six weeks later, uprooted the posts and replanted them a few feet back to make space for another ditch.

Ruth loathed work projects and fatigued strategically to avoid them. She lay down in the grass when they were meant to be weeding, on a cord of wood when they were meant to be shoveling snow, and under a steel table in the kitchen during a hot cross bun marathon. She pulled her kerchief over her eyes and listened for evidence that her brothers and sisters were getting to know one another unselfconsciously.

Clamor and fuss were merciful to the Shalom.

With a running start, Kurt Ayler rode the squat, wheeled A/V cart into the kitchen, fiddling nimbly at its knobs and harmonizing lustily with the Highwaymen.

"There's a lyric in this song," Ruth said from beneath the table.

Lotte's feet tipped up on their balls. "Did anyone else just hear a lazy goat?"

"There's a lyric in this song," Ruth said, just as loud and twice as buoyant, "where they sing that *the devil put his paw on the little tailor, with his broadcloth under his arm*."

Her audience indulged her, or at least listened.

"And," Ruth added, "it sounds like *with his butt-cloth over his arm*." Rhiannon Scholl was still young enough to snicker at such bait. The rest of the Shalom sisters were disappointed. Rhythmically they turned and pummeled buttons of yeasted dough against the table, clockwise, until the seam disappeared and the button became an unbaked roll, eligible for resting under a damp tea towel until four.

Ruth lay beneath them and the song continued. All thought and none remarked that Ruth was correct about the lyric.

ONE WEDNESDAY MORNING NO BROTHER APPEARED AT 6:30. THE tables were set and the toasters plugged in. Sheet pans of apple crumble, left over from the previous evening's Love Meal, reanimated themselves in the oven. "Those dear brothers," Lotte said, scrubbing down a clean sink for fear of idleness, "are probably just exhausted after staying up all night rehearsing their Dance of Brotherly Gratitude."

Ruth picked up bits of grated cheese with one wet index finger. "They held hands and formed a great ring around the perimeter of the Dorf, then did the mayim until dawn."

AT THE NOON MEETING KURT AYLER STOOD AND ADMONISHED himself for letting the sisters down that morning. He had failed in egg duty. By his own diagnosis, this failure was a secondary symptom of spiritual torpor. He asked the Brotherhood if he might make a fresh start through the rite of exclusion.

The Brotherhood, speaking through Jörg, accepted his proposal. In the silence that followed, a lesser brother might have wavered and loitered like a dandelion, but Kurt walked right out of the Meeting Hall. Jörg retained the microphone.

"We must all keep Kurt in our hearts as he enters the little exclusion," he explained. "He is out in the desert with God right now."

Ruth imagined Kurt Ayler, in his cornflower-blue button-down and suspenders, trudging along a sand dune borrowed from a Tintin comic.

"And because Kurt is outside the church, we must pray especially for his protection from the spirits and the forces that will attack him."

Now locusts and desert pestilence swarmed Ruth's brain. Bug-crusted Kurt Ayler crawled toward an oasis, cornflower-blue shirt now flayed and faded.

Since Kurt's was a venial sin if it was a sin at all, the Brotherhood administered only the little exclusion. Kurt would have no chats or handshakes, eat meals alone in his room like a convict, and meet daily with various elders to palpate the dead node of his faith.

A week into Kurt's, Rhiannon Scholl asked for her own little exclusion. The request was spontaneous, concluding a Meeting in which Eugene and Yoona Park shared about their business trip to Grand Rapids, and this time Jörg was unprepared. Before the Brotherhood, he promised Rhiannon only that her request would be heard.

Ruth, lately pleased with herself for calling it "the little *exclursion*" under her breath, wondered what Rhiannon had to atone for. She would never learn, as the request was denied in the next night's Meeting. Rhiannon accepted the Brotherhood's inclusion and apologized for the arrogance of overestimating her sins.

The bolus of eternity came very close to Earth and hovered over Hiram Knultz. He was dying, he announced, and the community echoed.

Hiram's ten-year tenure as Servant had ended without controversy in 1976, and now he was called upon to pray at every Brotherhood and to counsel the young people seeking baptism. His grandson Benji was withdrawn from a plumbing apprenticeship to push Hiram's wheelchair; Benji fetched the microphone when Hiram wanted to share, and returned it to its stand when Hiram grew tired. The community professed gratitude for these full days and wise words. They spoke of the nearness of eternity as though it were a weather condition.

After dinner the Shalom gathered outside Hiram's window and sang him evening songs. Benji wheeled him to the window so that he could smile out into the darkness, and stood beside him until the Shalom turned in.

Weeks passed and Hiram did not. Eternity abated.


HIRAM KNULTZ WAS DYING AGAIN. HEAVEN DIPPED AND OPENED his eyes, now milky with glaucoma, to its glory.

He had never quite resumed walking, and now two Shalom boys joined Benji in the tasks of nursing. The Shop built a wheelchair in semirecline, an open palm of a vehicle in which Hiram could lie, weighted under blankets, for his circuits around the Dorf. He spoke at meals and Meetings, and to a new baptism group, of a grace overwhelming to the point of diffusion. He smiled, and Benji stood in the backlit frame of their ground-floor window.

January became February became March. Ruth supposed it was the nature of eternity to persist.

Ross Becker was inspired to move the Meeting outdoors on the day Ruth was meant to leave Gracefield. Blithesome May! Shalom boys dragged benches onto the lawn and into geometry inscribed in their hearts. They could not arrange anything less than perfect concentric circles.

The community assembled quickly, the Omas like ducklings in their bonnets and most of the children barefoot. Ruth sat in the back row and picked wet mown grass off her ankles until the first song.

Ross announced a birthday, and the birth of Oskar Dampf in Wheathaven, and then stood to read from his Bible. God commanded and Jonah fled; God cursed the getaway boat and so Jonah dove overboard to spare his shipmates God's storms. Still God would not release Jonah; He sent a safe room in the form of a whale's body, and here Ruth knew what to envision: red walls vaulted with ribs and a pathetic figure vomiting seawater.

Ross sat. "The story of Jonah and the whale is a real challenge to me to accept God's will in my own life. We think we can run away from Him, but Jonah couldn't get away from God even at the bottom of the sea," he said. The community reflected on this or was at least quiet for a moment. An ancillary mic was relayed through the crowd toward Ruth.

"Today we farewell Ruth Scholl, who will be leaving after supper to go to Milwaukee, where she'll be working with the Missionaries of Charity."

Ruth flushed under the scrutiny. She was expected to speak; she clasped the microphone and hoped that the voice on the sound system was not really her own.

"Thank you for this chance to go out and witness," she began. Since breakfast Ruth had raced faster and faster around a shortening track, repeating and refining her last words to the community. They must understand that she was leaving in failure, not defiance; they must understand that she loved them too much to humiliate herself before God-in-them.

"I want the strength to follow Christ with my whole heart, my whole body, my whole mind. I want to return to the community scrubbed clean of all my selfishness and arrogance." She had rehearsed several more sentences of guilt and confession, but now she panicked and looped. She couldn't get away from God, even at the bottom of the sea. Again she thanked the community, and then once more. Making frantic eye contact with Ross Becker, something deep in her lizard brain changed and she handed the microphone back through the crowd.

The Missionaries of Charity, themselves daily witnesses to the caprice and fragility of a novitiate's faith, were not even moved to puzzlement by her failure to arrive that evening.

# Edendale

Then, briefly, mercy eclipsed dread. Ruth was transferred to Edendale, the Dorf across the interstate. It was just a six-minute walk under the overpass to her new life, and all the objects of which Ruth had custody fit into a laundry bag and a shoebox. Gracefield and Edendale effectively operated as one community, with Shalom pooled and meals taken together whenever they could be taken outside. Still, Ruth's transfusion meant leaving home; it was a forced fledge, a challenge from the elders to demonstrate and tolerate generic obedient love as a Shalom girl rather than as a daughter.

She was installed in a new family, the Muellers. Charles was docile, a Shop brother with the regulation passions of woodworking and chess. Martha was confounding. She was always cheerful and yet never laughed, perhaps saving that vulnerability for her husband. She regarded any provocation with caution, never curiosity.

Though lazy in her true duties to the Muellers, Ruth worked hard for Martha's laughter, but her jokes went unremarked upon. If not cleverness, then naïveté, she decided; she recounted the adorable behavior of animals and babies, and still Martha but abided.

Three days a week, Ruth was to attend the local community

college's program in culinary arts. The Brotherhood had chosen eight young people to take training that would better qualify them to serve. While the elders had been emphatic that credentials meant nothing to the Lord, there would surely be much to learn about fallen laws and human systems, and at the very least, these young people could make connections with the local youth and profess Christ in their school life. Ruth knew that the privilege of her selection was more important than the extreme miscalculation of her character it revealed. She was a terrible cook.

Kurt Ayler drove the students to campus and distributed their lunch money before they divided in commission: Kurt and his brother Obie to accounting, Tom Hauptmann and Arnold Wollmann to ag science, Berenice Stahl and Giddy Dettweiler to nursing, Ruth and Lotte Schmidt to the kitchen. They were meant to embark on their education in the spirit of a great commission, but Ruth preferred to think of the Ark.

During lunch break, while Tom and the Ayler brothers played pickup basketball and grumpy Giddy sat alone under a maple tree studying the Krebs cycle, Ruth perambulated.

She loved the campus. ICC—which rhymed with Frances of Assisi in her head, but was called "Ick" by everyone else—was laid out like a Dorf, pleasantly dictatorial in the journey permitted. The grounds were plotted along a French curve, with trim hillocks in which even a concrete administrative building could look nestled. Ruth found it impossible to feel lost. Even when she set off for Student Services and ended up in the dazzling squash court bunker, she knew she was never far from a campus map in which she herself appeared, a red dot, "here."

For the first time in her life, she was freed from greeting. In the community, salutations were reflexive, and everyone bade everyone good morning as they circulated the Dorf; Ruth had sometimes greeted trees when tired or preoccupied. On campus, she could go unrecognized for hours, inducing a near narcotic sense of invisibility. And who, amid the spectacle of worldly pursuits, would notice a girl in a modest dress and head scarf? Human shapes conglomerated in the grass; a sociology student offered a Hershey bar to anyone willing to take his survey; three girls Ruth's age rehearsed a dance routine, without musical accompaniment, in the shaded dell identified on the map as the Beekman Memorial Scholar's Grove. She could not fathom the confidence with which each of these people performed their characters. Perhaps they were given scripts every morning, and by resolution of some obscure clerical error Ruth might begin to receive hers.

PAUL FICARELLO SHE LOVED UTTERLY. HE WAS A GIANT, SO BIG that he exerted his own gravitational pull, and even Ruth, skeptical of bodies, found herself wanting to nuzzle him like a dog.

He lurched in late on the first morning of Modern Concepts in Pastry. "Young ladies," he bellowed, "together we will march right up to science and say: Let us eat cake!"

He was their guardian and guide through the spiral-bound course packet, a collation of twenty-seven recipes prepared by the American Council of Domestic Scientists in 1943 and promptly entombed in history. Council president Meredith Mooney, a bovine moue in a black-and-white cameo on the first page, guaranteed that with mastery of the twenty-seven "pillars," even the most timid bride could turn out enchanting rolls and pastries. Enchantment: How close to magic might Miss Mooney tempt them? Just last month the Brotherhood had been riven by debate over perceived satanism in *Fantasia*. There were deeper demons to cast out, but still.

Promising to tolerate bickering but not sabotage, Chef Paul assigned partners and made instant friends of Ruth Scholl and Kim Modelski. Kim was a creature of extreme visual interest, decorated with swags of fabric and a tackle box worth of jewelry, but just a single modest pearl nestled in each earlobe. Ruth moved to the back of the classroom, to a chair at the foothills of the mound of belongings over which Kim presided.

Within their first day together, Kim told Ruth: that she had known they would be paired; that she was studying Culinary Arts at the behest of her father, whose capacity for hospitality had died with his wife, and whose diner Kim was already managing after classes and on weekends; that the only difference between her and her twin brother was that he had been to California; that she couldn't keep her mouth shut; that her boyfriend, Scott, had given her the earrings, because pearls were her birthstone; and that Ruth's birthstone was—here Kim paused to perform an emotion that had yet to debut in the community—diamonds.

Most of Ruth's reaction was to wonder if she would marry Kim's twin, and whether Kim too might join the community. Less pressing, but easier to ask, were questions about Kim's parents, boyfriend, and clairvoyance. Chef Paul had distributed scrolls of butcher paper, on which every young lady was to draw an elegantly balanced supper including table setting, beverage, and condiments, so as Ruth filled an entire soup bowl with ballpoint pen (blue ink for tomato soup), she also prosecuted the most naked investigation into a non-member that her narrow life had thus far allowed. Kim was game; where others might hedge, she elaborated, furnishing details that expanded in fractal involution. By the time Ruth completed the last contour in her aerial map of applesauce (later mistaken by Chef Paul for a bowl of hair), she was sick with intimacy. She looked up from her drawing, and, absent a steady horizon, rested her gaze instead upon a herd of safely opaque girls at other tables. Kim caught her eye and smirked.

Ruth knew this was the bondage of secrecy invoked in Meetings, the lightless Christless covenant in which sin flourished like fungi. To experience it was to realize that some metaphors held.

KIM ACCEPTED RUTH'S INVITATION TO SATURDAY SUPPER, PENDING coverage for her shift at the diner and consultation with her boyfriend, Scott, who would be driving. This latter condition had not occurred to Ruth, to whom boyfriends were, like taxes and basilisks, notional. Perhaps even less than notional: her father could explain taxes and basilisks to her. But Kim would be Ruth's guest, Kim's sins and blunders Ruth's to answer for, and, since the community lacked the conditions necessary for any man to exist in the category, Kim's boyfriend would be Ruth's own ontological inconvenience to solve or finesse (this, in addition to the stated challenge of the evening: ventilation of their friendship and release from the shame of intimacy).

To the kitchen sisters, Ruth announced two extra diners, but to

Martha Mueller she mentioned only Kim, lying a means of wishing up until the moment her guests arrived. Waiting in the guardhouse, that evening manned by a Dettweiler mercifully absorbed in a pamphlet about silage, she allowed herself the fantasy of an indisposed Scott until the arrival of a hatchback the exact color and gloss of chocolate syrup.

Scott waited at the passenger door, watching the galaxy in propriety while Kim turned left and right before her compact mirror. Though his outfit disqualified him from every form of practical labor, in comportment he resembled Ruth's own brothers and the Brothers at large, all of whom, beyond a certain age, looked lost without the context of a mother or a wife. Kim alit. As in class, she was amply decorated, her skirts in perpetual motion. Scott could not, as she had hoped, pass as Kim's twin; their only physical similarity was the mild reflectional symmetry of their posture, holding hands in the tender conspiracy that Ruth recognized from engagement Meetings. The fact of Scott might resist finesse.

Ruth greeted both with her singularly impostrous handshake and then, aware of their witness in the guardhouse, set off walking. Kim produced (had been producing, would continue to produce) a melodious running commentary at which Scott only but always nodded and smiled.

They made an awkward three abreast through the dusk, toward the lights and life of the Dorf; Ruth could feel the dwindling of her chance to convey at least the law, if not the logic, that made a boyfriend impossible here. Every comparison she considered risked offense. Scott's position was not analogous to that of a king of a country no longer recognized by the community, and a boyfriend could not fairly be compared to other roles deleted from community life in efficiency or purification (mason, best friend).

Ruth knew herself to be an agent of criminal bewilderment and hated it; she was never sure when in her thought process to begin speaking, aware that she seemed to launch every idea from a nadir of intelligibility. What information did Kim have, and what did she need, to share Ruth's prospect on the evening?

"People might be curious about you," she began, employing the modal verb defensively, "but you don't need to say anything if you feel shy. Or if you don't mind a few people looking back at you like cows, you could say, I'm Kim, I'll be your waitress today. And then Scott—"

Ruth had been looking ahead to avoid being derailed by eye contact but here glanced at Kim and Scott and saw that they managed to walk while clasping each other sideways. Anxiety finally catalyzed a plan.

"Scott has been invited to sit with the college Brothers tonight—they always take the table at the back and talk about brotherly things."

"What are brotherly things?" Kim asked. And: "We can't sit together?"

It did not feel like lying at all; it felt like Ruth was revealing a much better version of the world in which she would not suffer. "I wish I hadn't told them, but when they found out a guy their age was coming they were so excited, and then the Servant challenged them to witness to you because they've had so much trouble making connections at school."

"What's the Servant?"

"The Servant is in charge of the community." For the first time she heard the words as an outsider might, and prayed she'd remember the dissonance at a more convenient moment. "Brotherly things, gosh. Soil erosion, small engine maintenance, and amperage are known brotherly things. Whittling. There's been a mania for audio equipment since we started using a microphone at Meetings."

"You'll be in heaven," Kim said to him. And to her: "Scott will be in heaven."

They emerged by the mail room. Everyone they passed hailed them, but it was the busy hour before supper, and the greetings were kept cursory. Ruth was relieved to see Kim and Scott split by the traffic; she steered them toward the Carriage House, from which Kurt Ayler had just emerged bearing stacked milk crates, one of mixed libretti and one of barbering supplies, crew cuts being administered on the first Saturday afternoon of every month.

"Kurt!" she called; correctly identified, Kurt froze and assumed a temperate air. "This is Scott, who'll be at your table tonight." Kurt had no cause to doubt her; by station, both only ever traded in secondhand authority. He expressed his handshake with a vigorous wag of his head; Scott offered to take the top box. Fearful of some sensual parting ritual, Ruth snatched Kim's wrist and walked her away from the boys, marveling that in the moment of commission her sins felt like mere shortcuts to the inevitable.

WITHIN THE COMMUNITY, STRAY INTIMACIES AMONG THE YOUNG people were cured with exposure. Two people in private could corrupt even discussion of the dinner menu; triangulation broke the spell.

Anyone would do for an invigilator, but Ruth hoped for a particular breed of gentle sister with whom to share Kim, and so headed to the Babyhouse; there was a half hour yet before the meal, and the Babyhouse crew would be cleaning the implements with which they'd cleaned the building. Ruth and Kim found ever-mild Hildegard Hauptmann, in huge rubber gloves, wringing rags.

"Greetings, Hilde!"

Hilde swiped at her face with the back of her forearm twice before Kim reached over to tuck a hank of hair behind her ear.

"This is Kim's first time visiting, and I knew she'd want to see the Babyhouse mop sink first." Hilde curtsied, and Kim returned the gesture without sarcasm.

"What do you use for the floors?" Kim asked. She explained her responsibilities at the diner; Hilde summarized the community's fruitless quest for baby-safe floor cleaner, and one clever brother's eventual invention of the formula now used on all North American Dorfs. Ruth succumbed to distraction, testing theories for why a full quarter of Edendale's babies had two-syllable names beginning with *S*, and by the time she returned to her surroundings Kim had given Hilde a tube of Avon hand cream from her purse and elicited a shape of smile rarely seen outside childhood.

The charm attack persisted through supper, where Kim sat with Ruth among a thicket of Muellers and made decisive work of her casserole in between accounts from Moody's Diner: the long-distance trucker whose courage during a grease fire earned him a lifetime of free meals, the little old man who salted and buttered his coffee, the two bunny rabbits her father bought from a produce vendor and had delivered with the carrots. What Ruth had assumed to be Kim's full anecdotal repertoire in class was evidently a random sampling from an endless supply. Watching the table surrender to curiosity, Ruth was excused from the shame she'd felt alone in; she had not been wrong to marvel.

Was it something in Kim's face? Robert Mueller, seven years old and precociously grim, studied her across the table with the intensity of a predator. Robert's refusal to laugh or smile had his parents in bargaining prayers since infancy; and yet watching Robert watch Kim, Ruth began to see faint reflections of her expressions in his face. His eyes widened with Kim's impersonation of her brother biting into a raw potato, softened as she skimmed changes in her mother's appetite in the six months between cancer diagnosis and death. Ruth considered her own chronic failure to induce sympathy and came to the provisional conclusion that humans were more vulnerable to feeling others' feelings than thinking others' thoughts.

Across the dining hall, Scott and Benji Blocher discussed with animation some subject lost on Ruth, the dynamics of which were illustrated with napkin dispensers and salt shakers and captivated all college Brothers present. Kim, beside her, had turned the searchlight beam of her own attention on Martha, whose predictable claims about death and its defeat were ennobled by the glow. For all Ruth's fears, neither Kim nor Scott had caused any confusion or offense. They were at home with one another, and in the world, and in hers; Ruth's envy was so profound that the only safe thing to do with her face was yawn.

The Shalom, enjoined to clean the dining room after Saturday suppers and then remain to interact freely among themselves, were that night to rehearse a section of a Haydn oratorio for performance at Jörg and Ursula's upcoming anniversary. Ruth extended the enjoinment to Kim, who demurred sincerely. As they waited in the cloakroom for the college Brothers to relinquish Scott, Ruth resolved to love Kim in all her superiority; in exchange for Kim's clear future as a recurrent guest, Ruth would pay any psychic toll, and gladly.

The Shalom began audibly sorting themselves by vocal range, and Scott emerged from the dining room, trailing farewells. Kim leaned in toward Ruth, one hand covering her mouth. "You've got to get out of here. You can stay with my family as long as you need."

RUTH SPENT SUNDAY STAGING DEBATES AMONG VARIOUS OPPO-nents as represented by her own mind: Kim, Gerda, her mother; Gods loving and wrathful. Still conflicted that evening, she was conspicuous in the rescue and consumption of two-week-old Leberkäse, so that a claim of indigestion would indicate discrete foolishness rather than anything contagious.

By Monday morning she was calm enough to waste the ruse. She rode to school with the other collegers and moved herself across campus like a piece on a board game, reciting newly introduced cooking vocabulary to crowd out nerves. Macerate, marinate, mignonette, mise en place, mother (sauce). Kim might request a change of partners; the mortification would be temporary, and surely preferable to a semester being pitied at such close range. Ruth had merely not to flinch.

Though the textbook predicated instruction on oven safety via a quick cheese loaf, Chef Paul began with an improvised speech

about camaraderie in the kitchen, context for his feud with the cafeteria staff and consequent inability to procure ingredients. Ruth
sat alone at her table in the back, whole heart absorbed in the reen-
actment: Chef Paul patiently taxonomizing the brigade de cuisine
for the cafeteria's Head Cook, whose title he pronounced at arm's
length; Chef Paul agog at vegetables steamed to the point of impo-
tence. When Kim entered, late and telegraphing deference, he
paused only to declare her knitwear marvelous.

Kim settled beside Ruth and could be heard rattling and rustling variously; Ruth kept her eyes on Chef Paul, now recounting
the criminal treatment of potatoes. A note edged into her eyeline.

> *Dear Ruth,*
>
> *I'm sorry for how Saturday night ended and I hope we can
> still be friends. Scott's cousin joined the Moonies so I know it
> can be hard to leave (if you want to that is!!). I am always
> here to talk about it but if you don't want to I understand.*
> *PS what is Chef Paul doing?*
>
> *Sincerely,*
> *Kim*

Ruth was suffused with endearment (the little footprints of the
double exclamation points, the premature postscript) and couldn't
help but turn to Kim and smile. It took the offer for Ruth to realize
that all she wanted was a friend who knew she was suffering but
would not make her talk about it.

CHEF FICARELLO'S HORROR AT THE CURRICULUM WAS AUDIBLE; instruction in the rudiments of baking was merely the substrate for an instruction in glamour. Very little did not conjure memories from his decade as *chef pâtissier* at the Monaco Carlisle. He described the palest blue fondant eggs in nests of spun sugar, centerpieces for the sixth birthday party of a child duchess. He replicated a black Bavarian custard he'd devised for the funeral of a sardine tycoon, then—though the class protested like a Greek chorus—demonstrated how the tiniest lick of spittle could collapse the whole chafing dish in an instant.

*Cornstarch is a fickle mistress,* Ruth solemnly transcribed.

It distressed her to think he might not know how much she loved him. She proved a terrible baker, and did not just ruin dishes but ruined them elaborately. Her custards were viscous, while her batters sublimated from liquid to cinder. Her tuiles contained the shells of both eggs and nuts. Extracting an especially molested meringue from the oven with huge paws, Paul Ficarello regarded her and the error she had created. "This, my dear," he said, voice gilded in affection, "this is shit."

She retained that phrase and its delivery for the rest of her life, though she never managed to repeat it out loud.

DESPITE HERSELF, RUTH WAS PIQUED BY KIM'S CLAIM THAT HER face reflected her astrological sign—though she doubted both individually, perhaps each could substantiate the other. Features of modular blandness rose to prominence in Kim's analysis; Ruth could see how her brow and cheekbone might indicate a martial aspect, how, beside siblings of the exact same stock, her particular ovine cast appeared an act of cosmic ordination. Kim, Kim explained, had the bright and delicate face of a Gemini. She surveyed Ruth the way men surveyed trees to be felled. Did Ruth, fire sign, blush, get rashes?

Chef Paul was late but audible in the hallway—a single, definitive "Cretin!" followed by the clattering of the ingredient trolley. Ruth knew she had neither time nor entitlement, yet longed for any tidings of herself.

On her next, recreational trip to the restroom, Ruth tilted her face and found new, pleasing planes; in the library she located a whole shelf of lurid purple books about the New Age. She copied out the zodiac on what she hoped to be the least conspicuous page of her notebook. She knew the occultic met with vigorous repudiation in the Brotherhood, which was well fortified against all and sundry forms of fortune-telling. It held no insurance policies, declined subscription to the *Farmer's Almanac*, and, in an annual presentation to graduating eighth graders (better known for its paraphrastic acknowledgment of masturbation), condemned astrology for the wonder it robbed from God. The movement of the Spirit was the only heuristic to which one might admit vulnerability, and all that ever forecast was her own resistance to it.

Ruth's curiosity was inflamed by deviance, and when she grew bored by astrology, it was only because it didn't work. The community's birthday book listed ninety-one other Aries, of whom she recognized two dozen, and in whom she could find no theme. While Ruth knew herself to be a quintessential ram (violent, hasty, choleric, impulsive, pioneering), Karl Krantz, born the same day four years before her, was a short and humorless Shop Brother distinctive only in his peanut allergy.

CHEF PAUL ANNOUNCED THAT THE EMINENTLY DIVORCEABLE Beverly Kamens, registered dietitian, would lead them into war against cholesterol in the Salads and Cold Entrées unit. Of course, of all things, Ruth excelled in the dark art of aspic. She became a dab hand at blooming gelatin and composing elegant ham rosettes. But more than anything, playing the mirror to Chef Paul's dancing light taught her the creative brio that made for a clever hostess. The inedibility of her creations was beside the point.

Yet as much as she adored him, Ruth proved a weak conductor of Paul Ficarello's charm. Reciting his edicts over supper at Edendale, she was ashamed at the Muellers' patient boredom. "He said that putting marzipan icing on his black cake would be rather like riding a vanilla Rolls-Royce to a honeymoon at Chocolate Hole!"

Charles Mueller descended upon his sausage to avoid responding, and Martha, terrified of all connotation, merely nodded back at Ruth.

For five months she had been their Shalom girl, and still she erred and hopped wrong during dinner conversations, into boring subjects and unchristian cruelty.

RUTH SET HER ALARM FOR 5:10, TWENTY MINUTES EARLY, TO visit the yogurt she'd prepared for breakfast and left in the walk-in.

Yogurt, an object of much magical thought on the Dorf, rivaled fertility as evidence of a sister's worth. With her inaugural batch, Ruth spared no superstition, stirring clockwise with a sterilized wooden spoon and cocooning the encultured milk in cotton towels. It would be a surprise for the Muellers, to whom she had so far proven a decorative nuisance. The cosseted yogurt was heavy, but Ruth was strongest at dawn and heaved it off the shelf—and onto her slippered toe. She yelped but held steady, and shifted the pot onto the floor. From the kitchen she kicked a dolly. On this humble craft she wheeled her yogurt out of the walk-in, through the dining room, and to the waiting stairlift.

She hoisted the pot onto the seat and hit the lift button with undue violence. Slowly she escorted her yogurt up the stairs, pausing on each step to encourage it, now nervous about the time. Martha liked the table set by 6:45.

At the landing, Ruth recalled the dolly. As she pivoted to retrieve it, the stairlift shuddered off and the pot of yogurt with it. It hesitated; then, with great malice, tipped over and down the stairs. The cotton towels unwound and the steel racketed, striking each step. Yogurt sprayed; the stairlift rails were coated. For several moments Ruth watched her disaster. Then she followed the yogurt back downstairs and began to clean.

She gathered rags and a bucket of soapy water from the cleaning closet, then moved from the top stair down, scraping dirt-marbled yogurt off each step onto the one below. On her wrist it was three minutes to seven. The pooled, hair-strewn yogurt repulsed her, but she stood to empty and refill the bucket.

Martha was waiting at the bottom of the stairs when Ruth returned. She took the mop and bucket from Ruth's hands, set them down, and braced Ruth in a hug until the weeping softened.

SHE HAD RECEIVED NO RESPONSE TO THE THREE NOTES LEFT IN Jörg and Ursula's mailbox. The first two were confessions of attraction to a certain young brother, the third a ponderous and insincere retraction. All three letters had disappeared into the Servant's realm, where they bloated ominously the longer Ruth waited.

After two weeks a pink note appeared in her mail cubby: Jörg and Ursula wanted to see her in their sitting room at ten. She told no one, retied her kerchief, and headed up the hill.

Jörg and Ursula lived above the Laundry building, the highest ground in Edendale. It was midmorning; the hall was dim and warm and deserted, the unattended dryers at full thrum. Ruth loitered on the first floor and read every available text: the laundry schedule, detergent instructions in English and Spanish, an illustrated limerick about lost socks that made less and less sense the longer she stared at it. Nor could she find meaning in Calvin's empty laundry cubby.

After ten minutes she walked upstairs and stood in the trap of Jörg and Ursula's house.

Ursula's African parrot minced back and forth in her cage. Ruth noticed that the dining-room chairs were stacked upside down, and that a plaid body was laboring beneath the table. Giddy Dettweiler, somber even rubber-gloved and on her knees, scrubbed forward and into view.

"Oma and Opa should be out in a minute," she said, replacing the chairs. To support Jörg and Ursula was a Shalom girl's highest piety. It was a job given as consolation to the hardest working and least likely to marry.

The Servant and his wife entered. Ruth rose to hug Ursula and shake Jörg's hand. They sat; no one spoke. Ruth launched into several sentences in her head. The bird bit at the metal bars of her cage.

"I didn't know this would be a Quaker Meeting," Jörg said. "You are worried? Jesus says, don't worry."

Ursula nodded. "Like the lilies of the field." Ruth noticed that her tiny feet, in wool socks and sandals, didn't reach the floor.

"Ursula read your letter to me. Do you pray for marriage to this brother?"

Ruth nodded.

"God knows your heart and will give you what you need. Do not pray for marriage—pray for God's will be done."

Ruth nodded again, familiar with the sentiment. Her internal thermostat kicked in; she felt broiled.

"We pray to God to answer our prayers, and He always answers. Sometimes the answer is no."

In Ursula's distinctive Austrian accent, the parrot began to squawk. "I love you," she skittered. "I love you."


THE LAMB OF GOD WOULD TAKE AWAY THE SINS OF THE WORLD. The recipe was easy enough, the real butter requisitioned from Stores, and from Paul the mold: an eight-inch lamb, kneeling feebly, cast in Polish tin.

Saturday afternoon the lamb unmolded cleanly. Ruth groomed a simple buttercream into licks of wool and stabbed him with the paschal flag, a satay skewer. Paul had suggested chocolate chips for eyes, but Ruth wanted realism; she tweezed two cells off a blackberry and nestled them in icing sockets. Too delicate for the Muellers' busy fridge, the lamb slept amid hundreds of Easter eggs in the walk-in.

She retrieved it in the dark of the next morning. Though one eyeball had burst and wept a violent indigo and the skewer flag flagged, Ruth was courageous; she snipped crude sunglasses from tinfoil, obscured her sin of ambition, and delivered the cake to the tolerant Muellers.

RUTH WAS RELIEVED WHEN THE ELDERS CANCELED HER EDUCAtion after one semester. She was needed in the office, Gerda explained, and would not return to school after the Christmas vacation but would instead support with stenography and archives. Gerda had plainly scripted the conversation, presumably in anticipation of defiance. She seemed unprepared for ambivalence.

"Anyway, it wouldn't have been the same without Chef Paul," Ruth volunteered, preoccupied. "He's going on a sabbatical in the Florida Keys." This he had announced at their end-of-semester fête. Dress code: "I will be bedight in my finest, young ladies, and hope you will too." (Ruth stuck a tinsel bow on top of her kerchief.) Paul served flambéed Christmas pudding and delivering an unrestrained soliloquy on glamour. It was glamour, Paul had said, that called him to Key West.

Now Ruth regarded Gerda: the inch-wide margin of hair visible beneath her kerchief was striped with white and center parted. Her bafflement tipped into irritation; the parenthetical folds around her frown deepened. Ruth had a vision of Gerda in Key West, and in one sudden migraine flash saw that she could never convey the beauty of Paul's spirit to Gerda, any more than she could explain to Paul how, in Ruth's world, this humorless middle-aged woman wielded more power than an empress.

"You mustn't think your time at college has been wasted," Gerda persevered, furious. "God uses all of our experience to His glory if we let Him."

Ruth looked up from her lap. "Simone Weil said that life is the conversion of suffering into pain, and life in Christ the conversion of pain into suffering."

Gerda appeared to pray for relief from her temper. "Yes, well," she finally said. "We mustn't let religious language get in the way of our daily work."

Ruth deduced that she had said the wrong thing.


SADNESS GLOWED AROUND JACK STAHL: BY SEVENTY-SIX, HE HAD left and returned to the Brotherhood four times. His wife, Myra, remained faithful to her wedding vows and raised their twelve children in the community with and without his help. For all her sorrows, she remained His cheerful sparrow, and only had eyes for providence.


THE EXACT REASONS WHY JACK CAME AND WENT WERE RESERVED for the Servants; the community had only enough information to low softly in prayer for him. He spent his longest absence seeking work as a carpenter in Lupton. Shortly after he left, a brother returned from the farm depot with one of Jack's flyers, folded respectfully for the Brotherhood's consideration:

> *I have over thirty years experience in construction esp. drywall and insulation. Very fair rates, no job is too small, also available for painting, landscaping, septic work, general maintenance.*

The flyer was considered in silence.

They prayed and were led. The Davis family, of Davis Hardware in town, was reminded of a long-owed favor and discreetly offered Jack a redundant job in their lumberyard, where he worked nobly but circuitously for the community from which he had sent himself.

Though Jack Stahl always left in private, each return was celebrated with a Love Meal. Ruth had learned the term *anhedonic* just before his latest return, and would always define it by Jack's expression at that night's Meal. He ate dutifully of the roast beef, smiled when sung for, and as the evening closed thanked the Brotherhood for having faith for him when his own had failed. But his was at most a logy tolerance. Myra, though, radiated delight enough for the both of them. It was to her easy preferences that the kitchen had catered, her favorite songs hastily arranged. She carried tubs of Jell-O home that night.

JACK SEEMED LEAST UNHAPPY STEERING LARGE VEHICLES. HE regularly volunteered to drive the coach, and the Brotherhood obliged him. Group outings were invented so that he could drive, the Shalom a regular cargo.

One early, yellow summer Saturday, they gathered in the parking lot after supper. Kurt Ayler called roll (twenty-six unmarried accounted for), and they boarded.

Ruth sat beside Frieda Dettweiler, one of the Shalom's three Friedas, easily teased for the speed at which she blushed. Ruth stared at her and watched her cheeks mottle.

"I do believe your blood is showing, Frieda," she said.

Who would marry Frieda? She deserved to stand beside a brother, hand held; her sweet face could ably accommodate the shapes of love and motherhood.

The bus swerved and dropped into a ditch, rutted like a pig, and died. Screaming occurred, generally; from the highway came skids and honking. Only then did time resume. Kurt Ayler ran to the front of the bus while Ruth sent up silent prayers for delivery from curiosity.

Presently Kurt chose four robust brothers to push the bus from behind as he steered it back toward mobility. Peering, Ruth saw Jack beside the driver's side, worrying the sleeve of his cardigan but useless. The bus was righted, the four spent men reboarded, and Jack sat beside Kurt home to the Dorf.

Sweet, bloodlet Frieda was the first to start singing, a spiritual that survived their four-part harmonizing. The air grew cool and blue as they sang, then black, and after all others had disembarked Kurt took Jack by the elbow and walked him back to his wife.

THERE WAS A NOTE IN HER MAILBOX AFTER LUNCH, A SINGLE sheet folded in thirds and taped shut. She put it in her pocket unread, so that it might mellow, and returned to work.

Colleen Wollmann was over from Gracefield that week and working across from Ruth for the duration. Colleen's beauty was an embarrassment to the community, and from Dorf to Dorf she required vigilant censorship to protect others from lust. At sixteen she'd become cornucopic: hair and eyes and lips spilled forth, nearly vulgar in abundance. She was eighteen now, ripe for request, though the New Testament made no mention of age.

Ruth took Colleen as profound evidence of something or other. She wasn't envious, having long ago determined that her own appearance was merely sufficiently inoffensive, but the moral implications of Colleen's face were troubling. Beauty was an argument, but for what? Colleen never stayed longer than a season in any community, though none but the eldest ever addressed Colleen's danger honestly. She was beautiful; the Servants could say this in private, in disappointment, ashamed at their own ability to see it. The rest of the Brotherhood was grateful for silence, a cover for both reverence and fear.

Surely Colleen's soul was the real victim of her beauty.

Ruth forgot the note until that evening. Tired after a lengthy Brotherhood and choir rehearsal with the Shalom, she accepted without bridling the anonymous suggestion that she encourage Colleen with some small act of love.

Ruth snuck early into the Archives office and hid an origami turtle in her beautiful sister's desk drawer.

KURT AYLER, ELECTED SHEPHERD OF THAT PARTICULAR SINGLES Breakfast, offered a provocation after the blessing. Several ones were unprepared for two thoughts on God before coffee, and had already begun eating when Kurt withdrew his placeholding spoon from a Henri Nouwen compendium.

"I am with people who are poor in spirit," read Kurt. Benji Blocher set down his fork discreetly. "They teach me that being is more important than doing, the heart is more important than the mind, and doing things together is more important than doing things alone."

To whom could such a statement mean anything? It was as true and meaningless as a line of algebra. The singles paused, then resumed eating, unprovoked.

Ruth, seated beside Giddy Dettweiler, tortured her with a forkful of Marmite, swinging the glossy brown tusks toward Giddy's yogurt. The sun rose and the singles were spontaneously, unanimously sated.

Kurt looked around the table. "Well," he said. Only Benji still ate, and only idly, scraping egg yolk off his plate with a jam spoon. "Let's do the dishes."

"Isn't it more important that we be the dishes?" asked Ruth automatically. Many present rejoiced in laughter.

RUTH STARTLED AWAKE WHEN HER SONGBOOK DROPPED OFF HER lap and landed thunderously. Six clocks in a row on the wall of the

Meeting Hall announced the time at every Dorf, and in Gracefield it was nearly ten p.m. The community was an hour and a half into Kevin Groebli's Meeting about the cosmos, which, like its subject, lacked any orienting terminal point; his narration petered out two dozen slides in, and now the hall was silent but for projector clicks and an occasional "wow" from Kevin.

As penance for falling asleep, Ruth recommitted herself to the galaxy. She was lately of the conviction that art could be anything one saw with reverent attention, and felt powerful summoning it from afternoon sunlight and Vs of geese converging midair. Kevin's slides did not volunteer the same pleasure, so Ruth took it in finding earthly rhymes for each heavenly image: sugar scattered on a black countertop, a speckled rock in cross-section, a goat's iris. Charles Mueller emitted a snore, and Martha took his hand discreetly. The slides continued.

A throat cleared toward the front of the room and then Jörg stood, back to the screen.

"I want to share something that has been heavy of my heart," he began. "But first, I want to thank Kevin for leading this beautiful Meeting. We are so small, but God—" He stopped and appeared to reabsorb the thought. Like many Servants, Jörg was fettered by syntax.

Then, at a cadence betraying rehearsal: "I have come to understand that I have been cold and legalistic in my marriage, and I ask Ursula for forgiveness." The slide behind Jörg changed and Kevin apologized off-mic; the visible sliver of Ursula's profile through the crowd was still. "And I ask forgiveness from the Brotherhood, for the example I have set. We show our love for God by the way we love our brothers and sisters, and when I ignored my wife I turned my back on God."

Ruth had never seen a Servant seek forgiveness, and wondered who among them had been deputized to grant it. Evidently, the request had been rhetorical; retaining the microphone, Jörg named an evening song, after which all would be released to sleep. Like the galaxy, love for God was available in miniature all around her. The Meeting ended and Ruth trundled automatically through the night, considering without concern that she found the parallel more comforting than any of its parts.

DORF BATHROOMS WERE EQUIPPED WITH ROUND HAND-MIRRORS in which it was impossible to fit all facial features at once, because, though always an attractive hazard, mirrors were least dangerous when they were too small to drown in. Ruth was perplexed, however, to find no biblical parable correspondent to the spiritual risk mirrors posed, no Old Testament wife beset with lizards for catching her own reflection in a pan of water. (As was always the case in Ruth's attempts to prove such negatives, she could not be sure what lay waiting in Revelation besides the grotesque shark-toothed angel gyres that scared her from reading further.) Some were immune to the particularly evil strain of vanity cultured in the mirror, and the implications of the demographics seemed to Ruth significant but impenetrable. Men, mothers, the elderly, and stupid dogs were not captive to their own reflections; young women, babies, smart dogs, and all the birds she could catch to test were.

A photograph was the most dangerous mirror, a flat trap for

those susceptible. The single camera possessed by each Dorf was locked in the Steward's office and released only to document those things already known and endorsed by God: babies, baptisms, weddings. Couples were photographed in their first week of marriage and then again after twenty-five years, appearing in the interim as hands or laps, landscape for children.

It was the Steward who had the film developed, and his discernment that curated the prints eventually pasted into albums and hallowed by familiarity. His was a job with spiritual corrosion inborn, and as such, the Steward's term was capped. A man could scan images for anything inciting vanity or lust for only so long before losing his mind to what sinners might see.

FROM AN AMISH COBBLER THE COMMUNITY RECEIVED 213 WOODEN shoe lasts covered in pigeon droppings. Such a deal would surely be impossible among the Godless, Ruth reflected; how could materialism encompass both the grace and the insanity of the gift?

The Amish, it seemed, had disturbingly narrow feet. For three consecutive Saturday afternoons, the Shalom scrubbed, sanded, and dried the lasts, after which they were sent to storage.

RUTH'S BODY SHIMMERED WITH ERRORS. BOBBY PINS SLIPPED AND hid in her nape, her forearms bore parallel grill marks, and her big toe poked a hole through the roof of every left shoe within weeks of wear. Like her mother she was knock-kneed. Her hairs came out if she brushed them.

Just as she knew grace only by its absence, so did she only feel her body when it hurt. It rarely did; even teenage boys envied her pain threshold, so she resigned herself to clumsiness and let herself be harmed. To be informed that she was bleeding was a frequent and prideful occurrence.

Ruth knew she should be ashamed of this neglect; to treat a child as she did her own body would be abuse. It was not the liberating self-denial of the Desert Fathers. She was on the Dorf, not an arid plateau, and she pleased neither God nor man with her uncombed hair and bruises. When she prayed, it was only for the will to pray, or pardon for the animal powerless beneath the mind riding it.

Thus, all could see that Ruth wanted no responsibility for bodies; she was too arrogant to risk anything that might wilt or die or fail. And yet the Brotherhood let Ruth care for her father's body for thirteen days before it followed his mind into Heaven. A stroke; the ice on the Carriage House steps; and summons from Gracefield, a car through the night. She arrived in her parents' home before dawn and crept into their bedroom, curtained and murky, to discover Esther Scholl dressed, awake, and lying beside her empty husband.

Arthritis cast Esther as Mary, and Ruth, Martha. While a team of brothers did toileting, it was she who manipulated her father into soft clothing and wiped spit from the bristling rolls of his chin. She loved this work; but that someone might eventually do the same for her was disgusting.

LOVE PREOCCUPIED RUTH. HOW COULD SHE EVER TRUST THAT she had reached her highest register of affection? Snickers was her best candy bar until she tried Cadbury's; before Calvin, others had nauseated her with hope. William Wollmann, teenage son of Bob and Dorothy Wollmann catty-corner to the Scholls, had been child Ruth's nearest obsession. The thought that he went to the bathroom at all, let alone left artifacts of wet towels and toothbrushes for her appropriation, addicted her to sin.

Her mind revolved around William until the Kupp family arrived from Cedar Hollow, and then it was Eddie Kupp, followed by her sixth- and seventh-grade teacher, Martin Stahl. Each was the only feeling she knew, and each bracketed a reality incompatible with the next. But if she could not trust how it felt to watch Calvin, playing soccer badly with the Shalom boys, what could Ruth trust?

REUNITING WITH THE WESTERN COLONIES HAD PROVED ONGO-ingly litigious; though now estranged and relieved to be lapsing, the Brotherhood knew that no break in the body of Christ was terminal. Having emerged as the star of the steno pool, Ruth transcribed weeks of secret negotiation between Jörg and Jakevetter, the Colony Servant. She typed quickly, spelled well, and retained enough Hutterisch to translate Jakevetter's grumbling. She had her own cubicle and a set of heavy, mushroom-colored headphones lined in Ultrasuede. At the end of each day, she delivered transcripts directly to Archives.

THE GUTS OF THE DEAL SURPRISED HER; UNITY OUGHT BE A blessed dissolution, not a contract. Jakevetter's conditions prohibited radios, ball playing, wristwatches, lightning rods, bed courtship, sale of Sunday milk, and bicycles. Little girls were to wear bonnets. None were to wear buttons, ride horses, or otherwise allude to militarism. The community would never know how much Jörg ceded in pursuit of Brotherhood, nor how little he asked in return. There was treasure in that field, apparently. Jörg made no petitions; unity was worth every concession.

Ruth already knew many of them, having crocheted the regulation five bonnets and sewn plackets into her blouses. Other changes were enforced through tacit deletion and selective memory. Bicycles were thrust back into fiction, deacquisitioned to a nearby youth center in one fell truckload. Any desire for a lightning rod went precluded. And despite Ruth's access, certain rules she could not parse, let alone question: Was "Sunday milk" any more than milk milked on Sunday? What on earth was "bed courtship"?

Jörg's sole request of Jakevetter's gathered Western Colonies came clearly from Ursula, who asked that their sisters adopt modest aprons, tight at the neck instead of at the waist. On the tape, Ruth heard Jörg grow impatient trying to describe the garment. "You will have your sisters send us the pattern," Jakevetter said with finality.

INSPIRED BY A LIBRARY BOOK THAT THREATENED TO IDENTIFY her calling in life through questionnaire, Ruth composed a personality test. It was purely and necessarily jest, as any audible calling could only be from God; nonetheless, she administered it covertly. She had grown absurd before Christmas, hiding her mischief in the cheer.

It was a February Saturday, and the Shalom were free for an hour before supper preparation. The Belgian youth choir long scheduled to perform that night had suddenly canceled, stricken by food poisoning in Flint, and so the Shalom inherited entertainment duty. Kurt Ayler, fresh-shaven in perpetuity, assembled the young people and solicited ideas. None poured forth. Kurt furrowed. They had just last week unveiled the Silver Moon dance to the community, he reminded them, and on such short notice could not possibly choreograph another by that evening. But boldly Kurt assumed he spoke for all the brothers when he offered to select and sing some Manx fisherman hymns in four-part harmony. Saturday supper was solved, and the sisters were free either to pursue joy or to change into clean outfits.

Ruth gathered six sisters under the dogwood tulip. They sat in a circle, no tuffets but the cold dry grass.

"Search within yourself and answer these questions honestly," she instructed. Frieda and Berenice Dettweiler, young sisters with many brothers and a flock of tumbling pigeons; Lotte Schmidt; recently returned Rebecca Rhyner; Susanna Becker of the Ross Beckers, and Susan Becker of the Paul Beckers—all hung in the pause. Distantly, someone practiced a trumpet.

"Would you rather peel an orange or walk to school?"

Rebecca laughed her juicy, satisfying laugh, then indicated her choice on the scrap paper Ruth had distributed. Ruth continued, pacing.

"Answer yes or no to this statement: I am happiest on the day of April twelfth." Several snorted. "On a scale of one to three, how much do you adore buddling?"

Dorothy raised her hand, but Ruth slapped it back down. "One is you don't adore it, three is you very adore it," she said. Dorothy marked her paper and muttered that her question had been answered.

"What is your deepest, darkest secret?"

"Oh dear, Ruth," said Rebecca Rhyner, though grinning. Rebecca was a glossy, ursine sister with a thick French braid. Though born in the community, she had spent much of her childhood in the world, and returned from it invincible. Ruth loved Rebecca as she was meant to love everyone; she hunted Rebecca's laugh.

"You are each one question away from knowing your calling in life," she said, waiting for Berenice Dettweiler to finish writing.

"My calling is to supper," said Susan. They had spent the morning preparing a purportedly Belgian fish casserole, French fries, and mayonnaise for their guests. As there was no noon meal on Saturdays, even the most unhinged combination was appetizing by midafternoon.

"Susan, this is no time for levity," said Lotte, able conspirator.

"Yes, Susan, you mustn't levitate," said Ruth.

Rebecca laughed again. The Dettweiler girls lagged but laughed anyway. Susan gave an imperious sniff.

"Final question," said Ruth. She dove backward into arrogance. "What is your calling in life?"

Rebecca laughed a third time.

ONCE ENGAGED, A COUPLE WAS PURSUED BY A FLORAL ARCH UNTIL marriage. It framed them at every community meal, disappearing in between for misting and repairs in the storage closet off the dining hall.

To make a couple's floral arch was either privilege or punishment, depending on whether or not you were Ruth.

The trend for themed arches was brief but torrid. Tom Hauptmann and Rhiannon Scholl sat beneath an armature wrapped in hay and hung with ears of corn. Simeon Dettweiler and Leora Maerz, who taught the fourth grade together before engagement, got a homely arch of apple boughs, rulers, and crayons. When some dear sister proposed a hospital-themed arch for medical student Eddie Kupp, the reaction was swift and final. The community had strayed into worldly frivolity, and floral arch sisters should henceforth limit themselves to grasses, ivy, and the modest wildflowers that grew behind the Meeting Hall.

SATURDAY WAS DEDICATED SHALOM TIME; THE YOUNG PEOPLE had exactly one evening in which to be free with one another, and, thus terrified, sang or cleaned.

That night they sang, rehearsing a spiritual copied from the Cedar Rapids War Resisters newsletter, illuminated with doves and daisies upon entering the community's canon. Kurt Ayler sounded the pitch pipe like a referee, and yet seemed surprised when his brothers and sisters sang terribly.

He made semaphores; they were quiet. "Let's start from the top." He regarded his sheet music, his pitch pipe, and his choir, but could not find a fourth object to blame. Kurt had grown easier to embarrass in his new adulthood, and moreover sought baptism.

"Sopranos, I need more spirit when you come in," he said finally, and made as though to resume conducting.

The Shalom was exhausted, discouraged, and vacated of the spirit. The vast window of the Meeting Hall, which in daylight framed a pastel tree line, was now a black mirror, behind which anything might lurk: cat, goblin, a rapist. Ruth had once attempted to convey her despair by means of a metaphor about windows at night—the bright room the mind, blind to all but its own reflection—and now added to it several meaningless metaphorical cats.

Another toot of the pitch pipe, and again they sang. Beside Rebecca Rhyner, Ruth warbled without vigor. Rebecca sang mightily; if her voice was beautiful, it was first and ever true, and she sang as though rebuking the devil with each pure note. Kurt stopped the song a second time.

"It's not working," he said. He turned away from the scallop of Shalom and took a few steps toward the window. The cats watched him pace.

Ruth watched the banner of the crucified Christ, a Renaissance reproduction hung from the highest oak rafter and dusted by extension ladder. She had thought little of it before—had taken as decoration this and every image of a loosely wrapped, bleeding man—but now she stared and waited.

Earlier that afternoon, while the rest of the Shalom dug up a hedge for fun, Rebecca had found Ruth weeping on the cow path. In the room Rebecca shared with Berenice and Frieda Dettweiler, Ruth sat on one bed between two stacks of clean laundry and looked at old photographs while Rebecca boiled water for tea.

"The first winter after they moved me to Sugar Valley, I cried every day."

Ruth was studying Rebecca's childhood, where the stout, kerchiefed girl looked just as immune to emotionalism as the woman bustling before her. What could have afflicted her?

"It was like living in the bottom of a soup bowl," Rebecca said.

"Despair?" asked Ruth, accepting her mug. Rebecca seemed to her the kind of sister pained only by inefficiency or foolishness.

"Sugar Valley," Rebecca said. "It's in a valley, and gets about eleven minutes of sunshine from October till March."

Ruth came to the photos of Rebecca in high school, here feeding flower-crowned Oma Doris as she lay bedridden, here grinning through green greasepaint, a witch in some morality play.

"I used to struggle with being single."

It was not a matter of if, but when, two sisters exchanged the female confession. The most generous interpretation, that one desired marriage for the sake of marriage, admitted entitlement, ingratitude, and distrust of the God and community in whose grace marriage was given. Ruth was a cynic; she had wanted not just marriage but marriage to specific brothers, and assumed the same shameful greed in her sisters. For whom had Rebecca hoped?

"Have you ever been in love?" Ruth dared. She had never asked anyone this question before, and worried that it was, if not entirely unchristian, at least worldly.

Rebecca sat cross-legged on the flooring and regarded the hem of her slip. "I thought I was," she said downward. "But I realized it was just a feeling." True love, even children knew, was not a feeling but a commitment; the dictionary had sent Ruth from *infatuation* to *fatuous*. "I used to be so jealous of younger sisters. When Tom and Rhiannon got married at the New Year's Meeting, I could hardly look at them."

Ruth had been there. Rhiannon Hauptmann, then still a Scholl, was only seventeen and bloated with youth. She and Tom had a son and their own Shalom girl before Christmas the following year.

"I kept arguing with God, blaming Him."

Ruth nodded. It had never occurred to her to blame God, when the elders were so much closer and more loathable.

"That night in the Meeting, I just kept thinking: Why don't I get anyone to love me completely? And then I heard a voice, saying, 'Aren't I enough?'"

Ruth, who had until now been preparing her face for sympathy, hastily regrouped to appear surprised and yet trustworthy: she would suspend all judgment if only Rebecca would elaborate.

"I never heard anything like that before, but I knew it was Christ on the Cross, speaking to me."

"Did you—" Ruth stopped and closed her eyes, testing sentences in her mind. "Was it a comfort to hear that?"

"No," said Rebecca, suddenly cross. Had it been a foolish question? "Christ didn't die for my comfort."

Ruth was entirely ashamed.

Now she stood beside Rebecca, waiting with Kurt to hear voices.

PRESENTLY AND WITHOUT EYE CONTACT WERE THE SHALOM GIRLS challenged to surprise the eldest single sisters with a meal and an evening of games. On a Thursday night they gathered to prepare three chafing pans of enchiladas and twenty-seven fiesta parfaits; secret the meal into the Babyhouse kitchen; and compose invitations and skits for those single-hearted sisters too old to toil after sundown.

Though herself long spent, Ruth invited each superlatively dear sister to appear costumed as her own hero. "Salutations, dearest Marjolein!" Ruth did salute eighty-four-year-old Marjolein De Jong, in calligraphy and in life, for her stamina; with her brother, Gijs, she had fled safe Holland for hostile Germany to join the community in its early years. While Gijs married and with his Carla begat bunkbeds of De Jongs, Marjolein remained in other people's families. When the Brotherhood chose Gijs to shepherd the first Australian Dorf, Marjolein received her own apartment, Shalom girl, and pet iguana. Nowhere did God or the Brotherhood promise parity.

"Your assemblage requested for a heroic Love Meal. Sisters to the Babyhouse, Babies to the Sisterhouse, and a complement of South of the Border orders, fun, games, sistership, sisterplane, and sisterautomotive."

Ruth planned to attend as her own hero, an egg; this she offered to Eleni Becker as they wrote and scrolled invitations on the cool swept linoleum of the dining hall. Eleni, last week transferred from Gunston, giggled kindly.

It was nearly ten o'clock, but the Shalom girls conquered night with industry. In the kitchen they sang as they worked, their spirituals unanchored by male voices. They passed to and fro in the bright doorway, rolling bins of shredded lettuce and ground beef.

"I'm going as Winnie the Pooh," Eleni said. Her kerchief had slid off and hung like a scout's kerchief round her neck; her ponytail looked defeated.

They had finished the invitations now and should have rejoined their sisters in the kitchen, but Ruth, crazed with restlessness, wanted desperately to know something new or secret.

"If you could wake up tomorrow on any other Dorf, with no jet lag, where would you go?" Such was the scope of a Shalom girl's fantasy. There was no wrong answer. Even so, preference led to sentiment, and sentiment to the anxiety that the bright clarity of the whole might be diminished by human favor for any one.

"Gunston," Eleni said finally.

Ruth hated the name and had always imagined Gunston a compound peopled by indistinct, misshapen relatives of the brothers and sisters she knew. Yet here sat specific Eleni, wishing to return.

"Is your family there?" Ruth asked.

The Beckers were a minor and modern tribe within the community. Eleni was young, still unbaptized, and might simply miss her own parents. Instead, she looked at Ruth and explained that she had been asked to leave Gunston for thoughts and deeds of impurity.

Ruth could not recuperate from this answer. She prayed God leach her of all curiosity, but He would not. He did, however, send Rebecca Rhyner to stand in the door and demand assistance assembling salad garnish.

"Want to capture some chives from the cutting garden?"

"Night chives," said Ruth. "We must steal them while they sleep."

Eleni laughed generously and so Ruth continued her babble.

They blinked through the kitchen and then back into the dark, following Rebecca's flashlight across the starlit Dorf.

"Who's your hero?" Ruth asked ahead. "Eleni's is Pooh Bear and mine's the concept of an egg."

"Oh dear," said Rebecca. "What does the concept of an egg wear? I'm going as Oma Anna when she was in the youth movement."

They arrived at the cutting garden, and Rebecca illuminated the sleeping chives. Eleni knelt and snipped while Ruth, extraneous, strayed from the light and stared up at the sky.

"I'll attach a yellow bowl to my stomach," Ruth said. Or cover a white bowl with yellow fabric; she would see what the kitchen sisters could spare. The costume room, though open to all, was useful only for those impersonating clowns, Victorian ladies, or centurions.

Behind her, the garden went dark. "Oh dear," said Rebecca again, with less exasperation. "What cranky batteries."

"Dough ear," said Ruth.

"You loon."

Eleni sounded as though she were still crouching. "Should I cut more?"

Ruth thought about vegetables growing Braille dots and said so. Rebecca resolved that they ought return to the kitchen. "Follow my voice," she said.

"And if you get lost just chirp like a cricket."

In the dark, their small conspiracy trundled Dorf-ward.

No yellow bowls were to be had, but Ruth's costume peaked in the telling rather than the wearing anyway. She wore a white nightgown rigged to billow, a white mob cap, and bare feet. Once dressed, she was confined to the Babyhouse with the rest of the Sisters, who would no more cross the Dorf in disguise than in the nude. Eleni was Pooh, Rebecca young Anna, Frieda Florence Nightingale with a paper tricorn nurse's cap atop her kerchief.

Many of the older single sisters appeared without alteration. Marjolein, though, wore rouged cheeks and an apron over her usual dress, and between spoonfuls of mashed potatoes—teeth too frail for the meal prepared—explained that her hero was "the humble sister."

With Calvin her imaginary audience, Ruth narrated a world of aggressive delight. All tedium and odium was redeemed when she could translate it to her idea of him.

Across the dining room, she watched the setting sun pick his face out of a group of Shalom boys. He glowed bright orange and squinted in her direction, and she felt everything, so much. Her stomach collapsed in tenderness.

For him she mocked the meal—spaghetti and vegetables suspended in eggs, an edible cellular diorama—demolishing it with the edge of her fork while Martha speculated about the hummingbird population. Ruth continued her telepathic monologue with a winning anecdote from the steno pool, wry but not cruel. She asked Calvin about the demands of discipleship. In deft digression from a character sketch of her father she quoted Edith Stein, or at least lodged a footnote where so to do; she thought at him far too quickly to transcribe any of it. If he loved her she would never have to return to a world in which any verb went unmodified.

The sunbeam moved on, and Calvin was shaded; now he could

see her staring back at him. Ruth blushed a hot and hazardous color.

RUTH WAS ASSIGNED TO SPEND HER SATURDAY MORNING CLEANing and organizing the Meeting Hall storage closet, which was better than digging fence-post holes (two Saturdays previous, a new paddock for Bumblebee the pony) but worse than mass production of flower crowns (last Saturday, May Day). The contents of the storage closet barely merited a milk crate, let alone a whole room: a dozen extra salt and pepper shakers, seasonal table runners, a tub of mismatched flower frogs, an empty tub labeled MEETING HALL ONLY DO NOT TAKE, and a boxed brass menorah acquired in anticipation of—here Ruth could only suppose—Jewish guests choosing to spend their Chanukah on an Anabaptist commune.

The closet was only ever entered to be cleaned, and so required no cleaning, but it served as a convenient holding cell for troublesome Shalom girls with no real work to do. Ruth was sitting on the floor, folded up so that she could rest her chin on one knee while reading, when the door swung in and Rebecca appeared.

"You nut," she said, voice half laughter, "what are you doing in here?"

Ruth held out her paperback: *Island of the Blue Dolphins*, which she allowed herself to reread once for every three real books she finished (two about the White Rose Movement and a biography of Corrie ten Boom with a misleadingly sensational cover). Despite her constant, lugubrious awareness of her own isolation, she envied Karana's life alone in the wild, with her whalebone hut and wild dog companion. Her illiteracy too, since reading was the most consistent cause of Ruth's loneliness, as well as its palliative.

"Come help in the kitchen. We have all this crazy fruit to unpack."

Rebecca had the authority of goodness. She'd already extended her hand to help Ruth up.

The community kitchen teemed with Shalom girls, all called from their respective Saturday morning jobs to receive a truckload of steeply discounted tropical fruit. A steel table had already been set aside for banana triage, with the overripe ones peeled and arranged in scallops for freezing. Frieda Dettweiler, clipboard in hand, circled a pallet stacked four feet high with boxes of limes, estimating a total count so high that she could divide it by the population of Edendale. "My own personal lime," murmured Ruth.

She followed Rebecca to the pineapple station, where the math was easier: one per household, two for households with more than four children at home. Rebecca scanned the laminated directory of Edendale families, frowned, and began to amend it in red marker.

The directory's format and shorthand revealed more about the community than any member would dare. People were grouped by household, and households by building. The entry "C M Mueller, 4 (1), + M Scholl, carriage house," for example, indicated a married couple with four children (one in infancy), plus an unrelated single person, living in a building too far from the inner Dorf for any member to hold a position of power. Rebecca crossed off names and rewrote them in a separate column: all the older, single sisters who, for their decades of humble obeisance, still followed plus signs in other women's families. To each, Rebecca assigned one whole pineapple.

"Pineapple sisters," said Ruth. Rebecca laughed and wrote it above the list.


WHAT WOULD SOULS WEAR IN HEAVEN? LILIES OF THE FIELD trusted in God and were clothed in His best; the community, surely less faithful, tried to answer the question in its own strength.

The original Brotherhood, exuberantly cresting Alpine scenes or flanking a wreathed cow in the few black-and-white photographs that lasted, looked like modestly free spirits: the women in long peasant skirts and blouses, the men in patched flannels. Wartime flight to America delivered them to denim, gingham, and several documented incidents of shorts; this was Ruth's childhood. She drew her stick-figure father and brothers wearing jeans detailed down to the rivets.

They adopted the Colony costume during the first unification and retained it through all subsequent struggles, obedient even in apostasy. Colony dress was the perfect insult to vanity, and as such, a great tribute to God.

The costume was biblically accordant and centuries in perfection. Sisters were composed of a pleated skirt and matching vest in a dark poly blend, white cotton petal-collared blouse (short-sleeved in all seasons), a slip, camisole, and underclothes. The complete outfit reduced any body to the vaguest of shapes. A soul was happiest when interred in soft, clean layers.

The sewing room was the most discreetly powerful of bureaus on the Dorf. Only sewing sisters had any say in who was to receive a new costume and exactly how unbecoming it would be. Citing economy, they ordered bolts from suppliers in perpetual liquidation. Lime calico; dun and deep grape pinstripe. From these they sewed costume after costume until the bolts wound down to selvedge.

All women's clothing was sewn on the Dorf but for the underclothes, which Stores ordered specially from a Mennonite supplier and emitted by the bushel twice yearly. For men, Stores bought denim and canvas workwear. Nobody cared, for men had no vanity, suffering lust doubly in exchange.

The sewing sisters worked vest darts like bellows to accommodate the relentless fluctuation of a fruitful community. They had little time for much else, and made only a few new costumes a year. A grown sister in good stead with the sewing room possessed three full costumes and a dozen kerchiefs, and demonstrated her preferred combination on Sunday. Fabrics were assigned and sometimes punitive. Capably preserved, most clothing lasted at least ten years; to receive an unattractive costume, therefore, might commit a sister to an entire decade of puce brocade. The thought of rejecting an outfit was unthinkable.

Kerchief semiotics were intricate and Dorf-specific.

ETERNITY SWUNG LOW AGAIN, THIS TIME FOR JOHANN DETTWEIler. It was clear what Heaven would gain: Johann was a hardworking brother, always chapped and smiling slightly to himself, descended from a legendary Swiss anarchist whose zealotry went still in Johann. As a young man, his was a nearly worrying calm, but young brothers had done much worse than declining to exit the passive voice. And then, right out of high school, he married Hannah Mueller, nine years his senior; an aberrational passion. She was a thoroughbred Mueller: clever, bowlegged, and short-tempered, but beside Johann she grew bashful. Five children were given in as many years.

They lived off the Dorf while their middle child battled a mutating affliction that began as dyslexia and ended in juvenile detention. The family survived, Hannah cleaning houses by day and babysitting at night, but Johann made no sense outside the Brotherhood. He simply lacked protective guile.

To host a demon required consent, and true possession was thus a joint effort between the possessing and the possessed. It was entirely plausible that Johann had welcomed his cancer like a guest, trusting it as he had the salesmen and Witnesses who appeared on his doorstep when the Dettweilers lived off the Dorf. At the time of its detection the tumor was described in terms of root vegetables.

His illness was announced during a joint Brotherhood, in which all the North American Dorfs shared a party line. More than a thousand brothers and sisters came on their knees to beg God for Johann's protection; this was not so arrogant as requesting He change His mind.

That evening the Shalom convened in the stairwell outside Johann and Hannah's home to sing evening songs. Ruth had lurked hopefully in the Help Yourself room after the Brotherhood, and arrived at the rear of a flock well into the fourth verse of "The Day Thou Gavest." She scanned for Calvin and saw his blond scalp, heartbreaking, toward the front; and she noticed that the brother singing beside her, jacket hood up but profile distinct, was Johann himself, having snuck down the rear stairwell to sing to his wife.

SOME DEAR SISTER HAD A VISION FOR EASTER BREAKFAST: ON each table a silver moss centerpiece, and at every table setting an egg-shaped candle inscribed with its owner's name. Luckily, the vision was granted well in advance, giving the Shalom three Saturday afternoons in which to make it manifest.

While the brothers were deployed to the forest to cull attractive moss, the sisters made eggs in the candle room. Threateningly competent Helen Wollmann led the project; though she had lived two years longer than Ruth, she had yet to err. Even Helen's poor eyesight provided an opportunity to wear the standard-issue community frames without vanity.

Ruth, a desultory candlemaker, volunteered herself to incise the cooled wax eggs with the names of every brother, sister, and lower creature in the community. She sat hunched in a corner, scratching cursive and muttering the same two lines of a May song. There were 328 names for 350 eggs, and she took full advantage of the generous margin for error. Compulsively, Ruth sought Calvin's name in the list. It wasn't there. Then she considered the least suspicious way to frame her question. "Helen," she said, afterthought of afterthoughts, "it looks like a few names are missing."

Helen was convinced but unprovoked by Ruth's performance. "We can only do what's given."

The high schoolers had taken on the preparation of the Easter breakfast meal, and were already swarming purposefully when Ruth entered the kitchen on reconnaissance. She feigned refilling the oat canister and then buddled conspicuously for three minutes, moving from station to station and teasing the high schoolers she knew best. The meal would comprise lamb sausages with fennel, rolls, raspberry streusel coffee cake, and wicker baskets of hard-boiled eggs. Ruth was more curious about the activity at the pastry station, where two sisters iced an unknown cake. Cakes served at breakfast tended to be quite meaningful.

Ruth approached Annaliese Wollmann, plucking rolls off a sheet pan.

"I am here to exact my Easter tax," Ruth said, as she detached a roll for herself.

Annaliese was a self-possessed junior girl with a port wine stain across her strong Hutterite brow. She played saxophone and could be trusted to indulge Ruth.

"Render unto Caesar," said Annaliese.

"I was wondering," Ruth lied, "if I could support the kitchen this morning. You know I am a professionally trained pancake."

Annaliese surveilled the room. "I think we'll manage."

They were silent for a moment while Ruth finished her roll. "What's the cake about?"

Annaliese was obedient to Ruth's tone. "No clue, I am but a mere schoolgirl." She could be good-natured into confession.

"You are but a seer mulegirl. Well." Ruth yawned and stretched her power over Annaliese. "An engagement?"

"I believe some dear brother may have a proposal for the Broth-erhood," Annaliese said, which she should not have. Engagements were nearly as rare as Easters in the church calendar, but they were secret; a protocol of double-blind preparation allowed the whole Dorf to support the couple unaware. The kitchen was often the first to know, for all change required catering.

"Thank you for your cooperation, my young friend," said Ruth to Annaliese, who turned back to the combi oven for another tray of rolls. Ruth glided to the pastry station, where Lisa Scholl and Lisa Stahl pursued sane industry. Both seniors, both seeking baptism, prematurely kerchiefed and mischief-averse; already they traded in the grace of prevention, and huddled to obscure the cake before Ruth could see it. She swooped away, paused at a laminated metric conversion chart, and turned back just quickly enough to see one of the Lisas place a marzipan trombone under a tea towel drop cloth.

THE WEDDING OCCURRED BETWEEN COURSES THAT EASTER BREAK-fast, the wild promise of marital eternity buffered by pastries. The young couple driving off into knowledge, the napkins wadded into cups, breakfast was over; by 8:15 in the morning every brother, sister, and child was back to work in the risen Christ. No reverent suspension could keep them from cleaning up. Ruth assumed her usual position rinsing silverware, then brought the balled tablecloths down to the Laundry and cried while starting the load.

With that, she curbed her emotionalism. She followed Martha around the Pinner's Loop trail in silence, too embarrassed to confess her stupidity. Martha exclaimed at each bluebell they passed. It was a beautiful, warm, wet Sunday. The Lord was risen, the Lord was risen. If only He would enter Ruth's heart, she might evict the part of her that suffered to realize that Calvin would not be tutor-ing trombone that afternoon.

Some sister had gathered up all the half-melted eggs and left them in a tub in the Help Yourself room. The pile dwindled for a few days and then disappeared.

SHE WAS IN CHILDHOOD, ON THE LIVING-ROOM RAG RUG, AT NIGHT. The grown-ups must have just closed a Brotherhood, for Ruth heard hushed and serious voices approach along the hallway; and then there was her father, holding James, seven, limp in his arms. Her heart beat. "Ruth," her father said, "James is dying. He took drugs and he won't survive the night."

James twitched and settled back against his father, tender as a dying animal.

"We must protect him from what is happening. He cannot spend his last night afraid."

Ruth woke sobbing.

HER PARENTS SAT SIDE BY SIDE AT THE DINING-ROOM TABLE, A thick ledger open before them. In this dream, she could read the entries easily from upside down and across the room. Names: Cal-vin, Benji, John. Boys she had noticed in middle school. Billy Yoder, a student at ICC with whom she had never mustered eye contact. It was a terrifying cascade of recognition, and then they were not just boys, but her favorite teachers, every elder, every Ser-vant. Everyone she had wanted to impress.

"Ruth," her parents said, in the dream, "you can't keep doing this."

SHE'D SPENT MONTHS POLLUTING THE ETHER WITH THOUGHTS for Calvin that he would never claim. What was the half-life for the psychic emissions of a twenty-year-old girl?

Upon returning from their honeymoon, the Calvin Winslows would live in a corner unit of the Carriage House, just the previous week vacated by an elderly couple conveniently rotated to a European Dorf. The Shalom spent all Saturday in a swarm of preparation: hanging new curtains, relining the wardrobe drawers, buffing floors untrod since last buffing. Ruth unpacked the crate of dishware and cutlery provided by Stores; though most families ended up with a motley cupboard, newlyweds received box-fresh matching settings, a luxury that in and of itself tempted many girls to marry. She had traded jobs with Lotte, who now had the plummiest task of all: making the sign that would welcome the couple to their new home.

Fragments of Ruth's secret running narrative for Calvin—tender, breathless, worthless—kept recurring unbidden. She stared vacantly at the silverware and husks of tissue paper spread across the counter. Beside her, a Shalom boy pumped a drawer open and shut to see if the slide needed lubrication.

"Can you do an uppercase cursive *G*?" asked Lotte, drawing at the dining table. "Or maybe she'll go by Birgitte now."

Waking from her stupefaction, Ruth turned to Lotte and wished desperately to lie. Instead, she went to look at Lotte's sign. She allowed herself one beat of self-pity, and then traced the cursive *G* required to welcome Giddy Winslow to her new home and married life.

THE TYPING POOL, IN WHICH RUTH PADDLED AWAY HER MORNINGS, was given the challenge to pare the community's songbook. It had grown bloated in recent years; what began as a pamphlet now ran more than three hundred pages, illustrated and clothbound and indexed by both title and first verse. Morning Songs, Autumn Songs, Songs for Rainy Days, Whitsuntide Songs, Hiking Songs. The most recent edition contained seven songs about the cuckoo bird.

Arguing to excise Love Songs entirely, Ruth repeated word for word an admonishment she herself often received. "Love," she blustered, "is a commitment, not a feeling."

Despite her bracing claim, in the end Love Songs were merely printed in their own book. Ruth was assigned to illustrate its cover—some carnal floral growth on a country gate—and did so with the deep proficiency of holy obedience.

THIS WAS THE SORT OF INFORMATION AVAILABLE ON THE BULLE-tin board in the Meeting Hall vestibule:

> *Peter Wyatt Wollmann, 7 pounds 7 ounces, born to Adam and Lisette in Gracefield, as yet unphotographed but represented here by a dear little blue-bootied illustration.*
> *Please return all emptied birthday baskets to Stores.*

*Tom Hauptmann seeks fellow rook enthusiasts to begin a weekly rook tally, for more information see Tom.*

In addition, the Men's and Women's Work Distributors posted Saturday work assignments for all in the community unblessed with offspring and so still at risk for idling.

Ruth stood at the bulletin board waiting for it to sprout news, delaying the dust mopping to which she had been unjustly assigned. Saturday morning chores rarely rewarded Ruth's particular gifts, as the Dorf needed cleaning more than wit.

Alan Feder, lately returned to the Brotherhood after three years in experimental apostasy, joined her in observing no news. He was purely medium in all qualities obvious from a distance, but his feline eyes and tan suggested the musk of the Continent. As a woman who was not his mother, Ruth lacked cause to speak to him, and so had communicated only in the perfect clarity of silence since his appearance at Edendale.

She reread the announcement of an upcoming meteor shower. The Feder family was a small clan by community standards. Ruth knew that Alan's parents began as Jewish socialists in Pittsburgh, predictably concerned about warmongering and private property before joining the community, and had produced five children of various ages and sexes. Only once before had she lived on the same Dorf as a Feder, when Alan's youngest sister, Sophie, spent eight months in the Edendale Shalom failing to offend. Ungenerous Ruth! Sophie had laughed at her threat to sew a forbidden pocket into the tail of her kerchief.

"Looks like I'll be going on the El Salvador mission," said Alan, still parallel at the bulletin board. "Just found out today." Ruth froze into a disguise of herself. "We're supposed to get back before First Advent."

And though logic, little dictator, indicated otherwise, she now knew when and whom she would marry.

"*Kolossal*," she said, like the group of high schoolers lately returned from their class trip to Germany.

It seems, dared Ruth, alone on her word processor during snack, *that Protestants regard moral law as an unattainable standard toward which we must always strive and always, inevitably fail—struggling to grasp infinity, we constantly perform the Fall simply by being ourselves.*

Opa and Oma had challenged her to put Christ at the center of her courtship correspondence to Alan Feder, so here she wrote.

*Consequently, the Protestants experience the law as punitive: for their sins, they suffer external or internal punishment, or both.*

In her last draft, returned with Oma's sparse marginalia, she had narrated a lively Shalom argument about the Iron Curtain. Personally, the matter compelled her to little more than consideration of metaphor—why was it called an iron fist in a velvet glove?—but to Alan she wrote of a God who knew no boundaries, the possibility of rehabilitation for secular communism, etc.

All licit courtship in the community was mediated by the elders. To an unwed, baptized brother confessing interest in a plausibly receptive sister, they might grant permission to correspond. To an unwed, baptized brother with only generalized desire, they might recommend correspondence to a slightly older sister on a different Dorf. The elders then read, edited, and delivered whatever correspondence resulted, guiding the couple through the platitudes of Christian marriage, waiting until both parties promised never to love each other so much as they loved God. At this point in courtship, the couple might be allowed to take a walk together, unsupervised. Ruth knew she was far from such access to Alan.

Beside her digression on the Holocaust, Oma had inserted a free-floating red question mark. Little could be rehabilitated from this draft.

*The Catholic understanding of law is more scientific, a structure that organizes and hierarchizes values in accordance with the fact that God is good. To break the law is not to do evil so much as it is to misunderstand the principles on which the world operates—like hurting yourself by touching a hot stove is not to malign laws of thermodynamics, just to misunderstand them.*

Still she had failed to mention Christ, the person of Him and how He might roost in their marriage. The snack bell rang distantly.

*But I ramble and know not of what I ramble. What is on your heart, Alan the Feather?*

She scrolled the sheet from the word processor and underlined *malign* with a ruler as the office sisters returned in flock.

RUTH LAY ON HER STOMACH READING A SOPORIFIC NOVEL SET ON a horse farm in Oklahoma, plotless but pacifying for it. Her brain rolled slowly down a gentle incline. She hummed. Berenice Dettweiler, a colleger training in accounting and Ruth's roommate that fall, did sums at her desk below a palm Cross and Psalm 139 in calligraphy.

Berenice was pious, rigorous, even her posture an indictment as she tabulated and checked her work. She returned from school at two thirty, studied until five, and then joined the civilian sisters in the kitchen for supper prep and excessive cleaning. Ruth, a mere typist after the aborted culinary training, had long abandoned hope of entering into conspiracy with Berenice.

Berenice hummed too, then didn't; the Shalom were cautious at humming, for though it had not been taken from them, neither had it been given.

"I was really encouraged by the Meeting last night," said Berenice, a hardy perennial who thrived in all climates and evidently took courage from middle schoolers singing autumn songs. Ruth, who preferred a general position of disagreement, was spared response when the hall phone rang.

It was for Ruth, chirped child neighbor Anke Hauptmann. Bad Ruth dog-eared her library book and answered the phone.

"May I speak with the brain of Ruth Scholl?"

It was Alan, after three months through the fine sieve of written correspondence.

"I'm afraid it no longer lives here," Ruth said.

He laughed! She elated.

"Are you on the right continent yet?"

"We just landed in Detroit."

She could think of too much to say. Overwhelmed and terrified of erring, Ruth lied to Alan, escaped the telephone, and returned to her room, where Berenice stared at her for a long moment as though fixing her in lunacy.

THE FIRST MEETING ALAN LED WAS A SUNDAY MORNING. SUNDAY morning Meetings were babies up, half-hour sprints of clapping songs and parables, followed by a break and then a Brotherhood. Alan had prepared a Gospel reading and a short list of finger games. He spoke down into the microphone, swallowing his words; Ruth felt a gutting proprietary tenderness from across the room, and could not bring herself to watch him.

On her first visit off the Dorf, her father had taken the family along to Saginaw to assist him in sourcing toothpaste. The expo was a dozen booths ringing the ice rink all weekend, targeting institutional administrators among whom the Scholls shone vulnerable. Ruth, five at the time, could not even organize her wonder; in the first half hour alone, she met cologne, pantyhose, paper money, advertising, and the smell of coffee granules under water. The rink populated and the building began to echo with scraping skates. Ruth's father submitted himself to polite conversation with a prison warden of distant acquaintance.

The children found Esther on a bench near the skate rental kiosk, where she'd darned a winter's worth of socks and now sat tatting. While James and Jeremiah pleaded to ice-skate, Ruth watched humans in their natural habitat. The rink lobby funneled skaters one way and expo attendees another, with Ruth and her mother sitting at the delta. She allowed herself to stare at passing men and women, but at boys she dulled her eyes and mimicked grim distraction. When a complement of cumulatively handsome teenage hockey players passed, Ruth had turned her whole body toward the expo, to observe instead an elegant lady eating a candy bar.

THEIR ENGAGEMENT LASTED THREE DAYS AND ENDED IN A DOU-ble wedding on New Year's Day. It was brief, even by community standards; she and Alan suffered only one Love Meal under the floral arch: meatloaf and parsnip mash followed by a raspberry Bavarian at war with itself. It was an urgent engagement, set at Godspeed, to accommodate Benji Blocher's incipient death; whenever possible, however briefly, all sacraments were availed to the dying young. An October diagnosis transformed the welding apprentice; any arrogance lent by youth and health was returned with interest, and by Christmas he was veiled in grace. These were full months for the Shalom, who shared his pancreatic cancer in all but the meaningful sense, and the entire community was inspired by his Christmas proposal to Susan Becker. Ruth's imp asked: What in bland Susan would merit a widow's dignity at twenty-five?

They said their vows at the morning Meeting, Ruth and Susan in matching garlands and different orbits. The Blochers were made first: Benji looked pale and papery as garlic beside Susan, but they were one, and each other's, and even Ruth ceded happiness. She would be married in a moment to the man holding her hand for the third time in their lives. They answered the marriage questions, ate peppermint cookies, and led the shivaree into the icy new year.

## Goshawk Lodge

Alan was prepared for marriage, deaf to the silence of it. He adjusted the rear- and sideview mirrors, checked the glove compartment for registration, and reread the handwritten directions to Goshawk Lodge before handing them over to Ruth.

"I am a very cautious driver," he said, eyes in the mirror as he backed up, "and I'm going to be focused on the road."

They left the front gate; they were off the Dorf, married before the eyes of God, with three hundred dollars in a nylon pouch and no accountability for a fortnight. Ruth devoted herself to Alan's profile.

"I need you to keep an eye on the exits. They've proved that the average driver is distracted from the road more than half the time, and that's a conservative interpretation of distraction." He grimaced, waiting to switch lanes. "I figure, knowing that, that I can realistically maintain focus eighty percent of the time. But factor in the other guy's distraction, and I'm still not happy with those odds."

Ruth began the story she always began on the topic of automobiles.

Alan interrupted. "Don't take this the wrong way, but I need you to let me concentrate on the road right now."

She said not one of the terrible things she thought, then. Her husband and his percentages were obscure to her. Two hours before, she had answered the marriage questions in blithe trust that Alan was the other half of her soul.

She thought about everything and kept an eye on the exits.

She became possessed by the image of herself, married, eating a slice of pie at the Round Top Family Restaurant. The image possessed her only after they'd driven by it, and she waited another two exits before sharing her vision with Alan.

"It would be so painterly," she elaborated, mistaking his distraction for doubt.

He silently eyed the rearview mirror and then changed lanes, shifting toward the exit without emotion. She squinted into her fantasy, trying to identify the pie on her married plate. And what would Alan order? Would she feel possessive at the waitress's curiosity? She imagined fascinating Alan. The turn signal ticked and he finally dared make the exit, but pulled over on the shoulder as soon as it appeared. They would claim their pies.

"Did you see what exit that was?"

Ruth had seen many things, and not that.

"That was one thirty-nine. I asked you to keep an eye out for one thirty-six." He spoke with taut patience or impatience and pulled back into the empty road. "Look for signs back south," her husband said. "Please."

SHE WAS MANIC WITH USELESSNESS WITHIN THE DAY; THERE WAS no work to do and no work to avoid.

She woke before dawn as a wife and watched Alan, sleeping in his T-shirt. Then and always, she regarded his comfort in creature functions with a combination of wonder and anger. He slept well, and guiltlessly.

She put on her housecoat and mobcap and commenced investigation. Goshawk Lodge was one of the Brotherhood's three retreat houses, providing privacy for the only instance when a young couple might need it. The freezer was stocked with steak and sherbet, the carpeted floor could not be buffed, and, between honeymoons, a team of Shalom girls was bused in to clean house and contemplate singleness.

Goshawk Lodge enfeebled the new bride. Even the table was already set; Ruth had been a Shalom just yesterday and knew how an act of malice could lurk in an act of service. She finally went out to the car and retrieved the spiral-bound atlas, whose pages she studied until Alan rose. He nodded at her, not unkindly, and set about making coffee.

Ruth was bored into boldness. "Did you request any other sisters before we started writing?"

He measured out the coffee with such precision that Ruth saw sums of multivariable calculus orbiting his head.

"How would you feel if I had?"

In confusion, Ruth defaulted to irreverent stupidity. "I would commit some sins."

Alan came toward her, braced her shoulders, and promised her that she had been his one and only request. She puffed out her cheeks to prevent expression.

SHE SHOT TWO ROLLS OF FILM ON THE CAMERA LENT FOR THEIR
honeymoon, which Alan returned to the Steward along with the
car keys and most of the money. Her pictures grew better and better the longer she waited for them; after three weeks, they risked
approaching perfection. The four prints that finally appeared in her
mailbox fell so far beneath expectations that she hid them in the
mail-room trash for several hours. They were rescuable, rescued,
and stowed in a messy banana crate under their marital bed.

In the first photograph, she and Alan stood holding hands in
front of Round Top. There had been no third party to photograph
them together outside Goshawk Lodge, so in the second she stood
alone, pigeon-toed, holding a twig and eyeing the camera with
grave intention. A picture of Alan standing on a tree stump, a picture of Ruth standing on the tree stump; as far as history was concerned, here concluded their honeymoon.

In high school, she had spent days' worth of hours in front of
the mirror, trying to figure out what she looked like. She would
leave class to stare at herself, willing her features to resolve into a
normal human face. They would not. The unified Ruth implied by
these photographs—the appropriate features, composed by the
same God who knew orchids and atoms—only suggested that cam-
eras were creative rather than documentary machines.

IN MARRIAGE RUTH CHANGED NAME AND LAUNDRY DAY. SHE
hadn't anticipated the shock, or shame, of mixing her own dirty

clothes with Alan's; it seemed to imply more intimacy than the sex act itself.

The first Tuesday she collected their combined laundry, she hid it beneath her family supper basket: cold cuts, sesame buns, red wax cheese, and bread-and-butter pickles the color of snot. This she wheeled directly home. She put their laundry away, pointlessly folding and stacking Alan's underwear; then, realizing that he would be at work half an hour yet, she returned to the closet. She chose a button-down shirt, slacks, socks, and his brown walking shoes, then laid them out on the sofa in human form.

She was in the kitchen repurposing some elderly green beans when Alan found her. He paused in the doorframe, squinting, still carrying his nylon briefcase, and Ruth thought: *My husband.*

"You did that?" he asked, tilting his head toward the living room. She looked down at the counter and nodded.

"You're a weird one, Mom," he said from the hallway.

# Cedar Hollow

The community came into possession of a stone manor house in the rural pinky tip of Leelanau County, Michigan. It had thirty-eight rooms, a cupola, and a dumbwaiter; it was constructed before the Depression by masons and carpenters shipped in from then-Crimea. The circumstances of the community's acquisition were as veiled as a soul.

Named Cedar Hollow, this fresh embassy for the Kingdom of God demonstrated the triumph of the inner church over outward appearances. Though it appeared a castle, it smelled of Cif and sauerkraut within a month of habitation, and careful colored-pencil pictures of babies and daffodils soon festooned the parquet walls. When Ruth and Alan arrived, exhausted from the performance of their honeymoon, Cedar Hollow was home even before they sang his favorite song at the welcome Love Meal or served her unseasonal stollen for dessert.

DR. TASSENARY APPEARED AT CEDAR HOLLOW ONE SATURDAY afternoon in darkest February, looking for all the world like a man invited. The community was but three weeks old, unprepared for visitors, but then, was Mary? Dr. Tassenary made no explanation but was greeted with warm confusion and ushered into the sitting room.

The community had just that morning read the story of the Good Samaritan, and all present felt personally indicted by the example; their Meeting ended with the resolution to seek sincere encounters, and to find evidence of God in every stranger's face. At this, Ruth imagined herself leaning over a low cot, grasping the gnarled hand of an elderly Black woman. She realized later that she had seen this vision before, in a fundraising appeal from the Sisters of Charity. But her mind could not have plagiarized a vision of Dr. Tassenary.

He was a tiny and turbulently pink little man, his hands softer than any Shalom girl's, and wringing themselves constantly. It was unclear whether he was nervous or insane. He stepped out of his loafers unbidden and hunched by the fireplace, his feet in their clean white socks turned in like fins.

Dr. Tassenary offered the name David but it retreated immediately and hid behind his credential; he must have hatched, homunculoid, with a doctorate and a lisp. A handkerchief bulged in the transparent breast pocket of a shiny white shirt. He was a man of eminent flammability.

Over the course of the evening, Dr. Tassenary did not ignite. He did, however, prove shrouded in esoterica. The community learned that while he instructed psychology at the junior college in Traverse City, he considered his vocation—"and I trust you know what I mean by that," said with gravid eye contact—to be the study of human excess. Here Dr. Tassenary recited verbatim the Brotherhood's teaching on property and sin. "You see," he said, flushing emphatically, "in the end, we become possessed by our possessions."

He had studied the Anabaptists from afar for decades, and in that time assumed a rankling, proprietary familiarity. Ruth wanted to stab him with questions. How could he claim admiration of their way of life but remain, content, in his? Did he think his fatuous catchphrases meant anything without the daily humbling of obedience?

"Ruth," said Corita, nimbly fording new shallows, "I'm sure that chicken could come out of the oven." Ruth excused herself for everyone's protection.

On the last, free day of the local Presbyterian church book sale, Ruth established Cedar Hollow's brief library; she and Alan returned to the Dorf with four failing paper bags of reading material. Thus within a single shelf she re-created the universe: a geology textbook without illustration, a promising bundle of recipe pamphlets that turned out to be Depression-era marketing for powdered milk, a coverless *Life* magazine guide to the Old Masters. It was this last item that provoked the question, suddenly pressing: Why didn't the Jews have any sort of artistic tradition? Ruth reflected on this mystery at Saturday supper, hoping to distract all present from her meal. She'd made too many wieners and arranged the extras in a heaped teepee over mashed potatoes. For all her culinary education, this monster was her sole Saturday supper contribution.

Wayne and Corita had spent the day having personal encounters with the pedestrians of Traverse City, so for a few hours the Feders served as elders of Cedar Hollow. Alan bore his responsibility casually, while Ruth had panicked over supper.

Dr. Tassenary was their only guest. It was no particular chore to please him, but Ruth was ashamed of the table she had laid, and so grew controversial.

"Is there even any Jewish music?"

Dr. Tassenary looked at her, tender in his perplexity. Alan excavated some mash. "Not now, Mom."

She suspended the question until they lay in bed, he reading Grisham, she watching him. "It would have been much more interesting than Wayne's story," said Ruth. Wayne had breached the breach with an anecdote about accidentally drinking a shallow dish of ketchup, having mistaken it for tomato juice. Ruth still could not think of a single work of Jewish religious art.

Alan kept his eyes on the novel and told her he really didn't care.

She got out of bed, went to the bathroom, and watched herself sob silently in the modestly face-size mirror.


THREE DAYS AFTER DR. TASSENARY'S VISIT, CEDAR HOLLOW received a letter from Traverse City. The single typed page, titled "Tassenary Soup," comprised a cryptic list of ingredients and a proviso: "I received this recipe from a Carmelite nun, quite coincidentally in Carmel, California, although she was originally from Mexico, I believe. She told me that it was a blessed recipe. In any case, I make it frequently and to rave reviews from colleagues—it has become my potluck specialty!"

Corita, dutifully grateful, copied the recipe onto an index card and clipped it in the clothespin beak of a duck that Wayne had carved for their fifth anniversary. Dr. Tassenary never recurred, but his soup loomed and proliferated in community recipe boxes for years.

THERE WAS A PALL OVER THE 1980S; THE WHOLE DECADE FELT like late afternoon in late fall, ominously dark too soon.

Ruth crocheted the first eight squares of an afghan in the dark, watching a public television special about the AIDS crisis that one of the brothers had taped to VHS; one of several plagues for the community's prayer and consideration. Ruth was pregnant, and would presently tell Alan.

The Brotherhood was looking outward in those years, sending young people to volunteer in prisons and in warm, poor countries. Shalom girls wrote letters to Third World orphanages, almost erotic in their sympathy; a pair of younger brothers even went down to Cuba for medical school, returning only at Christmastimes to tell about the spotless training hospital and the dignity of poverty.

Many young people didn't return at all. Later, the leadership would seek forgiveness for neglecting the inner church in these years, for putting the glory of worldly service above meekness and humility. At one Meeting, a plump Becker with the chafed red hands of a kitchen sister stood up and accused herself of arrogance for wanting to work as a nurse in Biafra. Ruth rolled her eyes.

The AIDS program had upset her, though, gave the world a new dimension in which to prove sinister. Ruth was riveted by the interviews with several men living the gay lifestyle in New York City. She didn't understand quite how the disease worked, but its effects on these men terrified her: in interview footage, there was only a delayed gray blur where their faces should have been.


THE CHURCH, UNSLEEPING, ROLLED ONWARD INTO LIGHT. WITH Dorfs on four continents, their vigil was constant; God's glory could not go even an hour unrejoiced at. The community had never been as big or as prosperous.

But to spread without sprawl or conflict was a task that lay heavy on Jörg's heart. Thus came the installation of an international tie line, and the subsequent occasion of their first Global Brotherhood.

Early morning in Edendale was lunchtime in Hazel Vale and late evening in Lonewood. Each Dorf assembled even earlier than usual and sang; each feared being first or last to dial in to the big empty conference in the sky. By the time Cedar Hollow connected, several of the North American Dorfs were already singing tinnily over the Atlantic. Dorf by Dorf they joined the song.

How distant and pathetic and magnificent it felt to be united by the tie line! Many ones were crying. For the first time since the Great Crisis of 1939, the whole Brotherhood sang together. During the Second World War, they had numbered fewer than two hundred convicted adults, and had met quietly in barns and basements. Now thousands of voices swelled. Ruth searched the sound for those she loved most.

Jörg spoke first. "My dear brothers and sisters, it is a great joy to be here with you." His voice placed Ruth back in her childhood, when he was just one of several deacons and participated on human scale. He had never frightened her, his English still childlike, his height mitigated by his gentleness. Now he held the monopoly on God's demands of the Brotherhood.

Each of the Servants announced their Dorf, offering many many greetings, and then Jörg read the letter he would send to the Vatican, pleading that they join together in condemning the American death penalty. It went unwondered how he wrote so elegantly.

That was that, all seemed to realize, and with duties rolling globally, the Brotherhood sang "The Day Thou Gavest" and untied.

THESE YEARS OF REACHING OUTWARD GAVE RELENTLESS PROOF that the odd seemed particularly easy to reach. Invitations to supper, extended countywide, yielded only two replies; from Dr. Tassenary, his regrets, and from Traverse City's church-run day shelter a lagging yes. On his predecessor's letterhead, Sam Bobbett accepted their offer on behalf of three young charges, proposing a distressingly late eight o'clock arrival to which the community immediately acquiesced, leaving Ruth and Corita three days to assemble a pauper's Love Meal.

A diminished envoy arrived seventeen minutes late: Sam Bobbett, tentatively bearded; a long, surly teenager named Jack; and Hector, a Black man who smiled and winked when introduced. Wayne and Corita interred whatever alarm they felt, but Ruth stared. Hector stared and smiled right back.

Dinner, which had already commuted back and forth from the kitchen twice that evening, returned once again. Over the course of an elliptical three-day monologue, Corita had determined that nobody wouldn't like pork chops, mash, and a green salad. Strawberry pies waited in the eaves.

Love Meals, by definition, featured colored napkins and a modest, thematic candy appetizer. Neither season nor occasion suggested a theme that evening, so Corita asked for inspiration and, denied it, set for each diner a yellow paper napkin fan and four symmetrically arrayed wintergreen gumdrops. Such an unorthodox setting would never have occurred on a bigger Dorf, but privacy relaxed Corita; in Cedar Hollow she was an appeasing host, only smiling conspiratorially when Jack wadded his gum in the napkin and sloppily masticated all four gumdrops at once.

But Ruth was riveted by Hector, seated diagonally from her and on his fourth plate of salad in ten minutes. He did not even feign interest in the other dishes as they circulated. Considering his salads, Ruth wondered if he was a Rastafarian, and whether that disqualified him from Christendom or merely flavored his faith. He ate rapidly but with extreme precision.

Corita asked many boring questions, avoiding homelessness. Biographies began at dessert. Ruth had no ears for Sam Bobbett's journey from social work to youth ministry, but stopped scraping pie filling across her plate when Jack began to speak: with audible, intimating passion, he described his calling to design light shows for music concerts. Ruth could not attach a single physical reality to his words, which suggested profundity; in a Brother, the same conviction was only ever summoned for profession of faith. Jack spoke about set lists, lasers, and dry ice. Ruth wondered how much of the love rightly owed to God was forfeited to false gods, and thought, *probably all of it.*

Hearing his own enthusiasm and wan with exertion, Jack went quiet. Wayne and Corita composed their faces, helpless.

Hector spoke at last, mercifully. His name was Hector, he repeated; God was good. All present were pleased with this line of argument, naïve piety being the highest piety. Ruth imagined a sepia church, Hector at the pulpit, the congregation clapping like birds in a dust bath. To dance for God! Her faith had nothing on his, imagined. Ruth seceded from reverie.

Hector was saying: God sent him to Traverse City to do His work, but upon arrival he could find neither shelter nor labor. Faithfully he began walking, at every corner asking God whether to turn or go straight; here Hector recited his negotiations with God verbatim.

"I said God, you want me to turn here? He said *no*, so I kept walking. Next corner I say, here, God?" His listeners were rapt in doubt and self-recrimination. Hector and God made miles of stilted progress across metropolitan Traverse City, until finally God commanded Hector to enter the side door of the church from which Sam ministered. He had been there since, awaiting further instructions.

Alan would not meet Ruth's eyes. Wayne cleared his throat and suggested that they sing some evening songs before closing. Jack abstained to chew gum, but Hector sang beautifully.

The dining room was cleared and dark. Down the front hall, under the Moravian star hung at the threshold, Wayne and Alan bade the guests good-night. Ruth could not imagine how men spoke to other men away from women. What could they exchange but practical data like rainfall and bus departure times? And yet the world was turned on conversations between men.

She and Corita stood at the sink, kerchiefs unpinned, Ruth washing and Corita drying the last of the dessert dishes. In the same room, going through the same motions, each occupied her own universe and had no desire to travel.

"That certainly was a lively evening," Corita announced, flicking her wrists over the sink. "You never know what to expect with these street people."

Ruth emptied her face. Corita, patience for encouragement spent, took off her apron and turned off the light over the sink.


ALAN SEEMED UNAWARE OF THE ABSURDITY OF RUTH'S PREG-nancy. In the first few months she wept often, and so often he would leave work early to read a chapter or two of White's Arthurian tales out loud while she lay on her back on the floor.

She was ashamed, and graceless in rejecting all but the most clinical concern. When once, chapter over, he asked whether she needed anything, she only stared past him and rolled over to face the wall.

"I am as self-sufficient as an egg."

She laughed at herself, but was angry at him for laughing with her.


SURELY MATHEMATICS WOULD CONFIRM THAT BEAUTY WAS EN-tropic; the prettiest tempera paints all mixed to brown, and the loveliest faces frequently go queer in combination. With every betrothal, Ruth imagined a monstrous composite of husband and wife, and after every nine months marveled that the resultant baby merely resembled itself.

She looked so often at her own face that it was just a placeholder in the mirror; she was a piece of paper onto which someone had written "eyes, nose, mouth," and perhaps "kerchief" in brackets. Alan's face retained some of its details; still, imagining their child, she saw only the fetal silhouette, nubbed and crustacean in the biology textbook. She could happily mother something like that—a blind kitten mewling in her skirt pocket—but feared a face that combined hers with Alan's would be dangerously neglectable.

She was not amazed by her pregnancy, she simply couldn't believe it. No physical symptom would convince her that her body contained two brains. Even as she grew round and sick with child, she knew that motherhood would prove her to be an impostor among human beings. The physical changes she ignored, sure that acknowledging pregnancy would suggest she felt worthy of it. While she waited for God to revoke the child, she swelled up like a zucchini. Her baptism and wedding rings would not even turn on her finger, and her feet lost their creases.

JAMIE WAS BORN AFTER EIGHTEEN HOURS' LABOR IN AUGUST, a fine purple boy. Ruth remembered blessed little of the birth except for her unhinged laughter when she realized she was straining to keep her face impassive while naked and violent below the neck.

Jamie stole her will to live and expressed it over a smaller surface area. Ruth faded while he gleamed and wriggled like a fish. She hoped that nursing might complete the vital transfer so that she could stop waking up in the morning. This she did not tell Alan.

He was a charmful baby, happy in every lap and quietly alert in Meetings. He ate and slept naturally; he cried only when Ruth knew she deserved it.

The intensity and ambivalence of her regard for him terrified her. She loved him as she was meant to love her neighbors, as herself; she often hated him.

This, too, she did not tell Alan.


THAT JAMIE GREW ASTONISHED HER. EACH DEVELOPMENTAL MILE-stone felt completely undeserved; she kept expecting him to deflate back into the baby she had created.

And yet they progressed through time as mothers and children always have. Ruth produced and Jamie suckled. He scooted, crawled, then walked. Although a Moravian star hung above each community crib, his first word was *moon*. Toward Alan he was churlish; Ruth he adored.

Corita, while they weeded, reminded Ruth that to relish the baby's preference would approach adultery as a sin against marriage. She spoke softly—as if Jamie, in a playpen shaded beneath the Wegners' single successful pear tree, were only feigning childhood and might hear—and forged into a new topic before Ruth could react. Had she any experience with transplanting tomatoes?

Corita needn't have feared the effects of motherhood in Ruth. Despite her infatuation, she had no instinct to hold her child, and nothing to say to him; his practical realities left her both agitated and bored. Like rising bread, seedlings, and world news, babies were dull as dun to watch for any length of time. Couldn't she just check in on his implausible development every few days? As soon as he was old enough to spend mornings in the Babyhouse, Ruth handed him off and returned to adoring him.

JAMIE WAS SICK ONLY ONCE IN HIS FIRST WINTER. HE WAS SENT home from the Babyhouse for quarantine, and howled in his crib while Ruth read in the living room. She was worryingly immune to the sound of crying. It was not that she didn't want to soothe him, but that his misery was so maddeningly far beyond logic. To his mind it was not merely an earache, but suffering without cause or end. Ruth reflected on this as he continued to howl. Did Christ regard her suffering the same way?

SHE EXPECTED THAT ROSE MIGHT BE ALAN'S CHILD, AS JAMIE WAS so notoriously hers. She wanted an equitable little family, a Punnett square of age, sex, and temperament.

Rose was mild and diplomatic in all relations, and slept well; Alan had taken to napping on Sunday afternoons, with Rose like a rock on his belly. Where Jamie's baby book was dense with Ruth's aphorisms and coded, postpartum argot, Rose's was, though written as from an infant's perspective, comparatively sane. "More blackberries, pweese!" below a photograph of her smeared in the orchard; "Summited Mt. Dad, enjoyed the view, relieved self." Beside, the picture of her last afternoon nap atop Alan.

In time, Ruth discovered that Rose had inherited Alan's small eyes and steadiness. She was confoundingly agreeable, forfeiting toys with all faith in bounty, and returned Jamie's frequent treachery with love. Ruth was discomfited to see her marriage performed in miniature.

THEIRS WAS THE NARROW WAY, THEY KNEW. COMMUNITY LIFE was a tightrope of obedience, and it was gratifying to watch outsiders struggle and thrash under church authority. They fled for as many reasons as they flocked. Arrogant young hippies, homesteaders, cultic refugees; they refused to die to their own will in such variety. Although of course, some dear sister clucked, what could be expected, the way children are raised now.

Few expected Theresa Sacks to last a week, let alone receive baptism. She arrived at forty-two, never married, a chronic weeper with anemia and aging parents. A simple assembly job in the Shop revealed weak ankles; typing gave her migraines. In desperation, the women's work distributor made her an honorary and burdenless Babyhouse sister. There, she sat in a glider chair and accepted infants into wooden arms. She did not sing when they struggled, nor swaddle nor sway, but only looked perplexed that a baby should move at all.

When honest with herself, Ruth found babies charmless and inconsistent. Her own were no better, just her own, and as such she forgave them in loyalty; but never would she prefer another woman's child to anything else that might fit on her lap. Still, in the

Babyhouse looking for a stepladder, Ruth was horrified to find Theresa staring into the middle distance while Todd and Gina's new Maureen pacified herself on Theresa's crooked index and middle fingers. She felt and hated Theresa's helplessness.

RUTH TAPED A LIST OF WORDS TO THE CABINET ABOVE THEIR SINK:

*Lively Unique Meaningful Beverage Turgid*

"Nice haiku, Mom," Alan said. He opened the cupboard for mugs while she considered her options. After lunch, sisters had until two before work resumed, although of late Ruth had discovered herself in bed well into the afternoon. Nobody seemed to notice yet, or perhaps Ruth had invented herself and never appeared in the Shop to begin with. As a woman or a thought experiment, she regarded her husband and his Thermos.

A better mother would take the rest hour to visit the Babyhouse. Ruth had tried, but felt ashamed at how much happier she was observing her children than holding them. Rose, eight months, was nearly back under the bell curve, and Jamie had apparently spoken several sentences to the Shalom girl on duty. How babies thrived without her! She spared them in depression.

"You can ban your own words if you like."

"That's fascist, Mom." He was getting fat; his father had been fat. The Feder men were typically lenticular by middle age.

Ruth agreed with her husband and went back to bed.

THE LAMBS LEAPT IN THE MEADOW, THE LARKS LEAPT IN THE SKY.
Spring converted Ruth into a cheerful obedient Sister as no psalms
could, and each day she woke with a deepening courtesy for life,
hers particularly. Beholding the morning often overwhelmed her;
to perceive the trees and the sky and the line where they met, and
all before breakfast, demanded more of her than any depression.

She rose earlier and earlier to maximize her wanderings. First
the Cow Loop out toward the front gate, then the long hairpin to
the Meadow House and back up through Help Yourself before
Alan even knew about the sun. Ruth risked observation only upon
return, when the first boys were sent to fetch milk or jam for a
mother who had gone to sleep without. As a mother herself, she
had doubtless moral authority in these encounters, and kept morning boys in the same category as morning cows. "Good day, my
young friend," she offered either.

She loved people so much on these walks, in her mind. Hover-
ing over the world, she prayed, continent by continent, specifying
her way home. With each petition she first pictured the face and
then made the request. For Rebecca Rhyner, gaping in laughter, she
begged God's consolation for thirty-four years of singleness. She
thought of her father in his wedding photo and prayed for a gentle
residence in Heaven. In prayer for Alan she found herself either before or beyond language, lucky even to summon his face. He was no
longer a man but the condition of marriage; the line between the
trees and the sky an optical illusion. She begged God to protect

him from herself. He always managed to sleep through her thoughts about him, and in that sense, her prayers were answered.

But Ruth could communicate none of her isolated, isolating reverence, and by breakfast the thought of others exhausted her for weeks.

THE SOUL'S ENTRY INTO KINDERGARTEN WAS ACKNOWLEDGED WITH the customary Schultüte. ("It's German," said Jamie to a jealous Rose. "It means school toot." Ruth could not improve upon his definition and so let it stand.) Stores supplied the contents; this year the children would benefit from a serendipitous closure of the Traverse City Woolworth's, from which Stores acquired a box of deadstock party favors in addition to the three pallets of gum-barnacled gondola shelving originally advertised. Ruth envied Jamie the novelties he would receive: glittering, zebra-striped pencils; an eraser shaped like a tennis shoe; a stout coil of fluorescent green plastic. Alan had taken the children out to watch the plumbing brothers operate a Ditch Witch; Ruth spread her bed with tissue paper and attempted to roll a cone around Jamie's treasure.

The next morning's Meeting was held before the schoolhouse: the Schultüten ceremony, three fall songs, and a prayer for Burgel Ayler, recently returned from a training in Germany on Fröbel's methodology and vocally devoted to fostering the childlike spirit in her first kindergarten class in accordance.

Ruth, by the rare and incontrovertible evidence of her own sympathy, knew the training to be compensatory. The year before, circa

Whitsuntide, Burgel had shown symptoms of being courted: she loitered in the mail room, sang to herself, grinned unabetted. Every summons from Edendale suggested imminent wedding, but each weekend she returned to them as a sister, not a bride. The grinning diminished. In August she'd been given a passport and the community's support to attend the training in Germany. Now, marshaling her first kindergarten into their classroom, could Burgel love and serve in public.

Jamie came home that afternoon and announced that his teacher was named Leg Rub, spelled backward.

RUTH LEARNED TO KNIT LATE IN LIFE, IN SECRET, A PRODIGY borne of duress. Even her first swatches were flawless, and with a single meter of acrylic, raveled and ripped out between experiments, she mastered gauge, ribbing, shaping, and finishing. It was a directed education: Jamie needed a sweater.

In readoption of the Western Colonies' rules, the community had acceded to a wardrobe devoid of buttons, snaps, or zippers. What could not be tied on was attached with hook and eye; thus did tedium court virtue. The sisters devoted an entire work evening to salvaging shirts, drinking Russian tea, and retrofitting a Dorf's worth of clothing in tacit irritation. With only four in her family, Ruth felt lucky; Annalena Hauptmann had eight girls under sewing age, and worse, one just old enough to sew poorly.

The following morning, Jamie was fastened into his jacket, and when he returned in only his undershirt Ruth had far better things to do than notice. He was bathed and fed and bedded before she wondered where the jacket had gone; but it was time for the Meeting, and after that a rare chance to shower, and then it was breakfast and her son without his jacket.

Where had it gone? Jamie, engrossed in a toast procedure, was noncommittal on the subject. Rose, flinching, was obviously complicit. Ruth appealed to Alan for support: "Dad?" Rose ripened for confession.

It transpired that the older boys had made a game of their new Colony jackets, fastening one's hooks to another's eyes and pulling apart to prove whose mother sewed best. Jamie's stitches ripped to Andrew Wollmann's, and he'd fed his ruined jacket to the furnace on the way to the wood lot.

Ruth knitted him a perfect, punitive sweater of baby pink yarn, three sizes too big and guaranteed to fit well into fifth grade.

On a Sunday afternoon in January, all community duties discharged, the Feders declined two hiking invitations and retreated to their apartment, from which to better admire the snowy geometry of the outdoors. Jamie, addicted to the Boxcar Children, sat ensconced in a duvet on the couch with *The Caboose Mystery*. While Ruth unpacked their basket from Stores (ground venison, baking potatoes, egg noodles, and precious sour cream), Alan put on the Tchaikovsky containing what Jamie called the "Evil Icicle Song" and balanced wet boots upside down on the heat vents.

Rose was silent, still perturbed by the morning Meeting, in which two Stahl girls in nursing school shared about their work placement at an old-age home. The filth they described was grim but predictable; it was the helpless elderly that moved many to tears. The girls spoke of men and women catatonic from neglect, or alert to pain alone; sick, scared captives pleading repeatedly to know why their children did not visit. Amanda Stahl spent an entire shift trying to bathe and toilet a bear-size blind man who had, two weeks previous, lain uncomplaining on a broken hip for more than a day.

Ruth set to making meatballs for their evening meal, and had both hands submerged in seasoned venison when Rose asked for help with her drawing. Jamie, selectively deaf, remained inert in the duvet; Ruth called for Alan, who presently returned from the bathroom and sat Rose on his lap at the table.

"What have we got here, Rose the Nose? Did you just draw this?"

From Ruth's vantage it looked like all art made before the age of reason, a nightmarish composition of spoked blobs, but Alan coaxed Rose into explanation: it was her, bringing a cookie to the old blind man. She whispered something and looked at him expectantly.

"That's a very kind idea, Rose. I'm not sure we have enough room, but I'll tell you what. Why don't I find out his name and then we can bring your picture to him? I bet that if we put it by his bed, the people there might treat him better. Because when they see this beautiful picture they will know that he has people who love him. Even if he can't read it, the love you have put into that card will let people know to treat him well."

Still somber but satisfied by the plan, Rose slithered out of Alan's lap and made to return her art supplies to their shoebox. Ruth was willing to sacrifice the last fistful of venison and, voice froggy with sentiment, asked if Rose would help her make the smallest meatballs in the whole world.

JAMIE WAS ACQUISITIVE, AND FILLED A CLEMENTINE BOX WITH HIS most prized finds: matchboxes, conkers, three steel nuts on a knotted twine, a monstrous tinfoil aggregate with which he tormented Rose. Ruth, in tender recall of her own little junk chest, did not interfere, even when a poached robin's egg went bad and smelled dead.

Rose related to creatures, not objects, and hoarded nothing. Had Ruth ever wondered about her daughter, she would have been disappointed to discover that Rose's dress pockets were confirmation: reliably empty. Nouns really were no more than slow verbs in her healthy little head.

WHILE LOOKING TOWARD CHRISTMAS, THE COMMUNITY INDULGED an otherwise latent Saxon gluttony. Cookie production spiked— *lebkuchen*, *pfeffernus*, *zimtsterne*—and the resultant ginger-anise mist lingered in the ventilation system for weeks. First Advent breakfast had its own dessert course. On every kitchen counter, a loaf of stollen lay swaddled like a baby.

Mid-December, the Shalom announced that they had been inspired to organize a Christkindlmarkt for the community. ("'Inspired' means someone told them to do it," posited Jamie, testing what Ruth would confirm. She did.) The German Christmas market was, like the civil rights movement and the birth of Christ, a collective memory of which no one at Cedar Hollow had actual experience. A search on the World Wide Web was sanctioned, and Stores enlisted to provide ingredients; the Shalom worked furtively all week, and on Saturday unveiled a transformed Meeting Hall.

The overhead lights were off, and an entire Dorf's worth of Christmas lights lit the grid of stalls. At the entrance, two girls with a stockpot ladled Glühwein in syncopation. There was bratwurst, a stall where the children could make ornaments out of red ribbon and straw, almonds roasted in sugar. A papier-mâché pretzel the size of an inner tube hung above the pretzel stall. The live Nativity featured a donkey borrowed with great fanfare from a nearby horse farm; recalling her own Shalom days, Ruth wondered whether this year's Mary had been warned against the spiritual arrogance that could result from portraying the mother of God.

There was no money exchanged, of course, but propriety proved regulation enough for the Dorf economy—a circuit through the stalls was intended to provide everyone with a full meal, plus embellishment. Ruth accepted a plate of bratwurst and took another for Alan, on switchboard duty that night. Though well within her rights, she felt conspicuous carrying two plates, and, both hands full, could not eat her own. She decided to deliver Alan his dinner early so she could return to the market unburdened, and sought her children to inform them.

Rose would be with Jamie, and Jamie would be in his pink sweater; Ruth scanned the Meeting Hall but did not see them. A Shalom boy rushed past her with a shovel (Nativity sanitation), and then from across the room she heard glass shatter and Rose shriek. The market tilted toward the commotion; Ruth considered placing the plates on the ground to better maneuver, but could not, hatred of waste countermanding even her maternal drive. She shuffled purposefully instead.

At the far end of the Meeting Hall she saw Rose, standing frozen among a scrum of Shalom girls with flashlights and dustpans: the familiar crawl of shard reconnaissance.

No blood, no wailing, catastrophe forestalled. "It was the Christmas pyramid," someone said mysteriously.

Figures shifted and Ruth saw Jamie, holding a tangle of red ribbon and radiating impatience with the adult admonishing him. Admonishment of a child misbehaving in public was the right and responsibility of all baptized community members, and in the absence of parents, the nearest adult inherited full moral authority. Ruth did not even consider parting the crowd to make herself known; the temptation to protect Jamie was chronic and futile.

Across the room, some dear Shalomer began "Greensleeves" on the keyboard glockenspiel, and the crowd dissolved on cue. Rose was evidently released from danger; she scrambled over, wound herself in Ruth's skirt, and made baleful hiccuping noises. Hands full and legs bound, Ruth could only wait.

Jamie seemed surprised that neither the telos nor techne of his caper were obvious to Ruth. He had taken ribbon from the ornament stall, tied it to a pretzel, and swung this around his head like a lasso. Why? His tone dropped from frustration into pity. To generate wind strong enough to extinguish the candle animating the Christmas pyramid.

"The Christmas pyramid?" What blinders had she been loosed from, this December night?

"The whirly thing," Rose offered from behind.

"It's that stupid contraption with the propeller on top," Jamie clarified, italics audible. "It *is* obnoxious."

Ruth knew at once what he meant, and that she had, up until that very moment, sorted the Christmas pyramid into the small compartment of familiar things without names (also: the groove between the nose and mouth, the pointy bit on the toothpaste cap). She tried to explain as much to Jamie, lately intoxicated by the thesaurus.

Again, he spoke as though she were the child. "That's the mush room. Mush room. You put mushy things there until you know what they're called."

The evening switchboard shift ended at eleven, and Ruth was asleep by the time Alan came to bed. The next morning, there seemed less urgency in confessing to him her inability to reprimand an intellectual superior; and by that evening, no point at all.

WHILE JAMIE AND ROSE WERE COMMEMORATIVE, RUTH'S THIRD child was named after nobody, on purpose. In naming babies, the community had long drawn equally from the Bible and the ranks of brothers and sisters graduated to eternity, but prosperity had accelerated the community's birthrate and exhausted a pool of namesakes growing ever more shallow—especially as experience in the public schools warned parents against creating baby Hedwigs and Herwigs. Oma Anna's death christened five newborns within the year, just one example of a coppicing effect that, though ingenuous, guaranteed confusion. By 1991, parents were challenged to consult the Holy Spirit for fresh inspiration.

The Spirit was evidently keen to counsel; the subsequent profusion of creativity cheered even Ruth, who had given up on loving words with other people. In 1992, the Cedar Hollow Babyhouse roster listed Ayesha, Caspian, Duke, Kira, Oliver, Savannah, and Skye. These, from brothers and sisters known to sigh lugubriously when read poems before Saturday supper! She remarked as much to Alan, who recommended Acts 2:4 and then changed the subject to the Tesla valve.

Ruth guessed wildly at the etymology of each new child, as the privacy of the naming process was, like every clue of life before birth, forcefully shrouded. The community had calculated all variety of heavenly metrics—Ruth had brooked admonishment for violations as petty as not opening her mouth enough while singing—but at the time of her marriage, newlyweds received no instruction on the creation or designation of babies. Jamie and Rose had been named at Alan's casual suggestion; in both instances, though she twitched and fumed at the banality, Ruth knew to assent. The alternatives were only differently boring. Names were self-fulfilling. This was not the appropriate theater for her assault on Alan's instincts.

Though incapable of imagining them otherwise, Ruth knew Jamie and Rose had been cheated. Her third pregnancy presented her first chance to name a baby anything she liked. That a name could reflect qualities intrinsic to a newborn seemed to Ruth a sentimental but insane delusion, and moreover she did not have the newborn yet; she was instead naming a novel cluster of symptoms, less mother than lucky pathologist. Without even gender as limiting factor, she set to coming up with her very best word.

The task delighted her; at all waking moments, and then in dreams, she sat in a small office in her mind sorting words into piles. She strove for a clinical impartiality to meaning—how else could one unlock the euphonic potential of words like Oven and Villainy?—and cackled in consideration of children named Flange, Antiquity, Vessel. She skimmed technical manuals and the catalog of the American Kennel Club's Centennial Dog Show, a hot commodity in the community library for which Jamie had waited three agonized weeks. Spaniel, for a little boy? Akita?

Every morning Ruth asked Jamie his favorite word, and when moved to respond he generated uniformly brilliant possibilities. He never questioned her curiosity, nor would its concurrence with her pregnancy have mattered to him; he still simmered with indignation that her last pregnancy had produced Rose instead of the homunculoid clone he'd requested, and had preemptive disinterest in whomever Ruth was making now.

Since transcription risked Alan's inquiry, her list of names was limited to what she could recite, weak candidates self-winnowing. Entering her third trimester, it stood: Hero, Kit, Minnow (from Jamie), Pekoe, Pip. The shadow list of names she could neither forget nor in good conscience use was longer—Booklet, Chickpea, Dud (Jamie), Glyph; Jam, Obelus, Slither (Jamie). The prospect of a human knowing itself as Chickpea—encountering the world girded with a word so perfect it was only fortified in abbreviation—appeared like a new point of light on her horizon. She need never reach it, so long as she kept moving forward with the possibility in sight.

AFTER HER DAUGHTER'S REQUISITE LUSTY CRY, RUTH LAY SWEAT-soaked, vision foxed and fading, and tried to recall her list. She closed her eyes. The creature who had until that morning possessed the quantum's dual citizenship was now definitively one thing—the soft, mild, pitiful, flexible thing—and audible, wailing in the arms of another woman across the room. A name occurred to Ruth. Rather, in the Brotherhood's terms, a name was given, their conclusion to centuries and synods of debate on effectual grace concentrated into one phrase now endemic; and with eyes still closed she called for her husband.

"You did great, Mom."

Alan squeezed her arm as if in assessment, and then left his hand in place, trapping heat and sweat where they touched.

"Do you need more water?"

Ruth shook her head feebly.

"They're just cleaning her up so you can hold her."

She shifted out of Alan's grasp and tried to burrow more deeply into exhaustion. "We could call her Idea."

In the silence that followed, Ruth soothed herself defending the suggestion to a version of her husband who could be bothered to articulate his disagreements. It would be unique in the community; it meant her favorite thing; it required only the slightest blunting of the mind to sound like it had been a little girl's name all along. And it had occurred unbidden, *despite* bidding, like relief from hiccups and most angels.

She fell asleep with one daughter on her chest and woke to another: Rose clung to the side of the hospital bed and fumigated Ruth with tuna fish breath (Alan's lunch repertoire minimal, mayonnaise based).

"Gretel likes me!" she whispered.

Ruth propped herself up on her elbows, triggering her hospital gown's garroting function and dislodging at least one of the devices tethering her to the array of monitors. Alan sat bassinet-side while Jamie dangled a homemade cat toy over the baby's face, narrating her plausibly scatological internal monologue.

Rose clambered into the bed with Ruth and all her tubing. "And do you like her?" Ruth whispered back. Rose's eyes were nearly black, pupils fully dilated with adoration, and her tone feverish: "I love her."

She did not know or ask what had inspired the name her husband chose. Having suffered the same identity theft, and spent all childhood envious of her own phantom, Ruth resolved to spare Gretel introduction to the idea of the daughter she had wanted.

A CHILD WAS NO LONGER A BABY WHEN HE HIT BACK. A CHILD was no longer a baby when he knew how to use a comb. A child was no longer a baby when his mother had another child. By this last definition did Jamie and Rose Feder quit their station, and by this last definition alone did Gretel Feder remain a baby her entire life.

FROM VERY FAR AWAY, AND WITH REMOTE FASCINATION, RUTH watched herself fade. Here, weeping at the breakfast table, hiding in her bedroom while Alan tried to get Rose in braids before school, leaving work to kill the afternoon with sleep. Here, watching her husband with effortless malice. Like the rest of her audience, she was powerless. Who could interrupt such an emphatic performance?

When Ruth became truly afflicted, they took her children, and then her cat. For weeks she refused to rise, eat, sing, or work. Barricaded in the filthy bedroom, she memorized the Book of John and wrote aphorisms on loose paper. When it became clear that she could not be uninstalled from her squalor, the community removed her dependents.

Alan, she kept. He rose earlier than other men—as early as Sam Mueller, the high schooler tasked with stoking the pellet stove before anyone was up to be cold—to rouse the children, make coffee, dramatize the day's Bible reading, sing a morning song, and eat his toast before pushing them to school in the laundry cart. Ruth barely had to sleep in to avoid the whole family. Once they were gone, safe from her at school and work, she could browse the breakfast remains, and from the living-room window watch the Dorf converge in joyful productivity.

Gretel, good and weaned at six weeks, had vanished entirely. Gretel, Ruth reflected, was the youngest Shalom girl in history sent to live with and serve another family; Clyde and Albertine Glanzer, with baby Blake just four days older, required only a change in their diaper rations to accommodate another soft-boned infant.

It was right for her brothers and sisters to act thus, she knew. She had neither deserved nor risen to the challenge of motherhood; given the best role in a metaphor for God's love, she had succumbed to her own mind instead.

Jamie and Rose still slept in their own beds, which Ruth, on better days, made between naps. She heard their murmured bickering before dawn, ate their toast crusts, and did not bother to ask her husband in whose homes they supped.

She asked him about the cat. Gustava suffered no more in Ruth's troughs than she profited in the peaks, for she was a cat. But her disappearance enraged Ruth, and on the fourth day that the kibble bowl remained untouched she kicked it across the living room.

Alan asked her to clean up the scattered kibble when he arrived home that evening. She was by then ashamed into stubbornness, and asked whether she wasn't even allowed to keep mice. She could not look at him as she asked this, for she had begun to cry.

If he suffered, Alan did not tell her. He brought her meals and took her laundry, and he prayed for her aloud each night before they slept. Now he sat beside the shape of his wife beneath the duvet and patted her lumpen form. "We love you, Mom," he said. "The Devil's not going to win this one."

FROM THIS REMOVE SHE WAS SUMMONED TO MARIO AND BAR-bar's house in the middle of an afternoon. She walked leisurely from the Meeting Hall, passing the third- and fourth-grade classes out on a science expedition; the students goose-stepped across the picking garden wearing huge tube socks over their shoes to capture burrs and seeds for taxonomy.

Barbar admitted her. From the couch Mario rose to his full, fitting height; Ruth realized she could recall no short Servants. Alan was five foot ten. Perhaps she should observe this to him at supper.

The whole couple, not just the mirror but the light itself; she was enough of a bother to warrant service unreflected. She sat and waited for their judgment.

"Ruth," said Mario.

Barbar softened at her. "Mario and I want to ask for your forgiveness. We have failed to support you and Alan, in your faith and in your marriage."

Startled, Ruth began to laugh. Barbar looked to her husband for guidance.

Mario handed Ruth a folded page. She opened it and saw it was a fax. "You have been invited to meet with Opa," he said.

Grace so overwhelmed Ruth that she wanted to touch the Servants. She half stood and staggered toward Barbar, who did not relax in Ruth's clutches.

"Well," said Mario. Ruth scurried back to the Meeting Hall in love.


At Moody's Diner, she sat opposite Opa Jörg. His summons was so urgent that she'd left the Dorf in her house slippers; when he noticed, on the drive to Lupton, he was delighted, and distracted the hostess so that Ruth could tiptoe in his wake.

He ordered from a waitress who had no idea who he was; this upended Ruth. The gravitational center of her world was a mere satellite in others'. She wondered what the waitress wondered, serving an old suspendered giant and a barefaced, barefoot young woman. She worried the knot of her kerchief while Jörg bantered.

Pie, sherbet, two cups of coffee. Ruth went to the bathroom and watched herself in the mirror until the door rattled, then lingered along a wall hung with snapshots, headshots, and signed menus. She located Kim in childhood, Kim in her waitressing uniform, and Kim in maternity wear at the sale of Moody's to a South Asian family; each vision caused a spasm of delight. When she returned to the table, Jörg grinned; a helpless mirror, she grinned back.

"So life is not so bad after all."

Ruth grew embarrassed. Something in him deflected argument, deflected even curiosity; she would say or suppress anything to keep him grinning at her.

"I want to be happy," she began. Where next? She had claimed this in so many admonishments, and it was true but still wrong.

However she said it, it bored Jörg. "You begin a sentence *I want*, then you will not be happy," he said. "You cannot be so friendly with the Devil. Think of your husband."

Ruth knew she did not want this parsed. Opa Jörg's intentions were clear.

Duly, she requested that the Brotherhood administer the laying on of hands. Within the week, the Feders were moved.

*Twin Rivers*

The generation born between her father and Opa was a distinct and troubling species. Many had come of age during exile in the jungles of Paraguay, where they were distorted by humidity, illness, and poverty. Until late in high school, Ruth had thought that the gargling Paraguayan accent was a side effect of polio.

Mary Marshall, called Mary Mars Bars to her confusion, was a child of Villa Milagro, the Dorf established in the war.

The Brotherhood had fled Europe on a refrigerated cargo ship, passage secured but destination theoretical. The *Aurelia II* arrived in Avonmouth bearing beef carcasses and departed with all three hundred and forty-seven members of the community. They stayed below deck, separated sexes by hanging sheets from meat hooks, withered, and stank; two children and an infant died. For five weeks they floated homeless, denied port down the Eastern Seaboard, and when Paraguay finally granted refuge, the Brotherhood could only accept. It became clear that the Paraguayan officials had optimistically mistaken them for Nazis. They'd sent a deputy from their own Fascist party to meet the ship; the man saluted Hitler as the Brotherhood disembarked. When he finally recognized the scale of the error—on the ferry to Asunción, he'd bragged about the docility of local peasants as though he himself had tamed them, to mute disapproval—it was too late to do anything but hide his German guests. The Brotherhood was offered seventy acres of un-cleared jungle in the Chaco, to share with snakes and jaguars and worms that burrowed through skin and laid eggs behind your eye-lids. This sick Eden they named Villa Milagro. Mary Mars Bars was the first baby born there to survive infancy.

Heat-cured by sixty, she could barely hold a broom. Keeping her occupied provided part-time occupation for three brothers: they built her a jig to make wire springs, a jig to stretch those same springs for another purpose, and a third to straighten springs be-deviled and uneven. Any indignity at days spent rotating between the three tasks Mary Mars Bars kept hid in her heart.

All who suffered childhood in Paraguay were marked and duly cherished. In 1993, a troop of those healthy enough—cradled and guarded by a larger troop of prime Shalom—were sent down to visit the abandoned Dorf and tidy its burial ground. In the Meeting recapping their mission, Mike Braun projected slides but said little. A photograph of the thatch-roofed Brotherhood room, collapsed and sprouting guavas; the Shop, where brothers had turned wooden bowls, unsellable, on a lathe donated by the Mennonites; Markus Hauptmann demonstrating that his father's well still drew; a mynah on the leaning, vacant bell tower; Mary Mars Bars stooping beside the grave where three of her younger siblings were buried after the fire.

THE UNLIKELY NINETIETH BIRTHDAY OF CYNTHIA BECKER occasioned much joy for all of Twin Rivers. Birdy, toothless, near blind,
Cynthia remained delighted to eat Tootsie Rolls and hold babies;
she had attained age without authority, a sure sign of a humble
heart. Having long reserved her only worldly curiosity for the
Amish, she received from the Brotherhood forty dollars, permission, and means to attend an Amish auction in Hillsdale. Gallant
Alan chauffeured, and Ruth sat in the back with Cynthia, watching
her hands dapple and then flare with the changing tree line. Cynthia spoke the whole way—to herself, hoped Ruth. Frets and spec-
ulations and a queer story about an Amish baby that knew to fold
its hands in prayer at three months. Neither Feder interfered with
the monologue; they attained unity in their marriage. Civilization
decreased, and then they had arrived in Amish territory, all dun
and dust. Hundreds of black horses idled at a long trough along the
road. In the adjacent lot, hundreds of black buggies waited empty.

"We should start making coffins on wheels," Ruth said.

"Don't be morbid, Mom," replied Alan, parking.


THE CHILDREN ON THESE PORCHES WERE DUSTY AND GRIM. Nu-
merous too; eight were staggered across the front steps of a house
no bigger than the Dorf's candle room, and glowered silently as
Ruth passed. Amish auctions were called only in times of privation
or acute tragedy.

One barn held livestock; another, household goods; and a third, women, children, and Band-Aid-beige folding tables of snacks. In the first, they watched a velveteen stallion sell for thirty-five dollars, and Ruth plummeted at the indignity. She escaped to the snack barn and wasted half an hour picking up various cellophane-wrapped lumps, inspecting their undersides for anything more interesting than a price. She could feel the surveillance on her skin; the low clucks of Pennsylvania Dutch stopped as she passed. The Brotherhood had occasionally loaned its own doctors to the Amish, but neither expected nor received reciprocal goodwill, and Ruth felt shame regarding herself from their perspective: spiritual weakness proven by forearms freckled from exposure. Even Amish babies wore rigid black bonnets with more structural integrity than a carport; she hugged her sides. Children lurked behind skirts and peered down at her from the hayloft. Only one boy, studiously feeding hay through the grill of a standing fan, ignored her.

Cynthia was gleeful on the return home; she had preserved her forty dollars to return to the Steward.

For Alan's thirtieth birthday, Ruth copied out her favorite Bible quote onto construction paper. A series of errors required drastic cropping, but she glued the resultant, more-or-less rectangular scrap onto a piece of card and trapped the whole thing in an envelope to preclude further damage.

With similarly conservative foresight she prepared an unremarkable breakfast; the occasion was no reason to pretend they needed anything but routine. They sang and prayed and ate their toast. Ruth gave Alan the secret gift of silence when his words irritated her. Jamie and Rose ate and fussed, oblivious. Gretel manipulated a handful of porridge across her high chair.

As it was not the job of Stores to delight thirty-year-old men, Alan's birthday basket was exactly appropriate. Sausage, bought salsa, a bird guide; Ruth would have bridled had the contents pleased her husband specifically. His preferences were the closest thing she had to private property, to do with as she pleased.

He opened her gift and withheld reaction. Jamie asked what it was, and he read aloud:

"Jesus answered and said unto him, Because I said unto thee, I saw thee under the fig tree, believest thou? Thou shalt see greater things than these."

Ruth spoke as though to her children, to delay rising insanity. "Jesus had a very good sense of humor."

Ruth's gift was returned to its envelope and lived happily, quietly, in the box where her husband stored everything she made him, and all of her poems he found in the trash.

HER UNDERSTANDING OF THE ELDERS WAS LIMITED AND WOULD always remain so; she was not the daughter, nor ever the wife, of anyone with power in the community. For all her distress at decisions made in secret on her behalf, she never envied the elders or their wives. Theirs was a heavy burden. At baptism, she had vowed to daily forfeit all power over others; those called to serve were duty bound to take up that authority again, to command their brothers and sisters, to carry the secrets of the Dorf in fairness and sobriety. Through an open door she once glimpsed Barbar, face in a rictus of sympathy, while Theresa Sacks sobbed out of view.

"We will never know why the Lord asks some of us to remain single-hearted," Barbar was saying, as was plain she had said often before.

FROM A CANDLE-MAKING CO-OP IN YAKIMA CAME DICK MCLEOD, a zealous toad of a man, raised Godless but ready to ignite in and for Christ. It was beyond comment that the community attracted able men and damaged women, but all maintained vocal gratitude for both. Within a year of Dick's baptism into the Brotherhood he married Iris Eicke, a narrow sister eight years his senior, and the two begat twins, twice over: first Thomas and Gabriel, then Anna and Beatrice. Ruth recalled one childhood Christmas breakfast when three eggs in a row bore double yolks, and prayed for the same for the McLeods. Should she suppress such prayers? Did they harm anyone but herself in God's eyes? Though Iris was a terrible cook and rumored to serve peanut-butter sandwiches at every private meal, the McLeods were a joyful Christian family.

Dick was a masterful tinker and smith, and bequeathed to each of his children one skill. Thomas he taught to whittle, Gabriel to work a jigsaw; Anna dovetail joinery, Beatrice inlay. In seventh grade the girls surpassed their father in secret, waking early on school mornings to craft him a walnut cigarette case inlaid with symmetrical pewter ducks. Smoking was Dick's toll for entry from the world, and Stores allotted his Camels without judgment.

IT WAS WIDELY KNOWN THAT ONE COULD DIAL OUT OF BUT NOT IN to Twin Rivers pool and sauna building. The only Dorf with aquatic facilities, Twin Rivers would not also be the only Dorf with aquatic calamity, and gave lifeguards no excuse for distraction.

The pool was open Saturday afternoons and all Sunday. Ruth, a resolute land animal, went only to chaperone bobbing otters Jamie and Rose. Merely being wet qualified as an activity; they gamboled to exhaustion and she didn't need to bathe them at the end of the day. Ruth had no memory of playing as arbitrarily as her own children did. She must have swum but it hadn't taught her anything except not to drown.

Mildly she watched her daughter. At six, Rose had earned her first swimsuit, a community-designed canvas romper edged in elastic and weighing easily five pounds wet. The same pattern scaled up to hide swimming women's bodies, although Ruth wore hers only in the sauna. As Acts omitted the pattern for modest swimwear, an internal bureau of her own dear sisters had invented the garment of necessity. The premise: the female form persuaded despite itself, especially when wet. Multiple layers of dark cotton were required to dampen its rhetoric. The difference between fear and reverence was semantic.

IN THE 1990S, THE COMMUNITY SENT FORTH YOUNG FAMILIES AS witness to the sanctity of life; Ruth, herding two littles and a baby, proved a telegenic Madonna. In this role as evidence, the Feders attended a weekend of pro-life fellowship in Washington, D.C.

She had never seen so many Christians together. They prayed over hotdogs and fruit salad, grasped hands and saw Christ in one another's faces. The children loved it; Ruth gratefully ceded Rose to a picnic blanket covered in Somalian nuns, the most beautiful women she had ever seen.

To a Baptist social worker she explained her kerchief, citing Paul, the whole time stinging at her own spiritual pride. The frequency and brevity of denim shorts perturbed her.

But she felt nothing about the unborn. She knew, logically, that each was a thought of God's, knit carefully at conception and no less holy for being hidden; but even her own children had felt unreal until they arrived. She did not weep at pamphlets like the dear Vietnamese gentleman from Bethesda, who pressed one into her hand and made tender, invasive eye contact. The photos looked like chicken parts to her. She'd looked down, smiled at the top of Gretel's head, and felt fraudulent.

At convocation, a squash-like cardinal spoke about the culture of death. "We must refuse to measure the value of a person by the suffering they might cause us," he said, and continued on about euthanasia and Down syndrome. Ruth stopped listening. She thought of her parents, Alan, her brothers and sisters in Christ; there was no tallying the suffering she had caused. She wept quickly and beyond the children.

RUTH HAD LIMITED INFORMATION ABOUT ITALIANS. WHEN THEY appeared in novels, it was typically to emote or dine al fresco. Consequently she offered little resistance to the theory put forth in *The*

*Latinate Soul*, a slim volume of "cultural observation" rescued from a bench outside the Kittson County Community Center. Ruth held that anything abandoned in a public space was not merely hers, but providentially hers. She read the whole thing in one sitting and could not wait to relay her findings to Alan.

The author of *The Latinate Soul*, Professor Leslie Maynard of Bates College, appeared nowhere on the book's jacket, and so Ruth did not know whether to attribute the ideas therein to a feminine man or a husky woman. She imagined a crude combination of the two, in turtleneck and tweed, interloping among Latinate souls: peering out from behind a prop newspaper in a Riviera café, eavesdropping on peasants while submerged in a vat of wine.

After this cartoonish behavior in Ruth's mind, Professor Maynard concluded that the Latinate soul—animating Italians, Portuguese, and Spaniards—was fundamentally different from the Classical Teutonic soul. Where the former was passionate, the latter was coolly logical; while the Latinate loved, the Teuton merely regarded.

Alan was ambivalent, which Ruth diagnosed as Latinate; a Teuton would not abide ambiguity. She confidently identified six other Latinate souls at Twin Rivers. She felt enlightened, recognizing in their gesticulation the same heat that ripened olives and tanned Caesar. And, observing herself observing her children, she forgave the vast absence of intuition; she loved them in theory, as was her nature.

On Rebecca Rhyner's forty-third birthday, Ruth was six hours behind, withstanding a typically peculiar Monday lunch of meatloaf, fried rice, and steamed green beans. If she repeated without interruption the limerick she had composed for Rebecca during the meal's digressive prayer, she might retain it.

The limerick, by formal necessity, told in cryptic shorthand a tale of the old man in the peanut. Rebecca had revealed him to Ruth decades before, in trail mix after their vigorous observation of a Shalom work project. Every single peanut had a tiny bearded man living in its cleft, Rebecca said, and laughed, and showed her.

Rose, laboring humbly on her rice, buffered Ruth from distraction on one side; Jamie, on her other, was winking in Morse code to Randall Mueller at the next table. Alan was on switchboard that afternoon, and so sat across the Dorf with his plate and novel, harmless to her concentration.

Rhyme intact, she fled lunch cleanup for the empty hall of the Carriage House. It would be darkening in Wheathaven, families would be singing evening songs in lit windows before the children slept and the adults met. Rebecca—for the past year assigned to serve the mischievous, diabetic Oma Helga—would be wearing her flower crown.

Ruth dialed switchboard and asked her husband to connect her to Wheathaven. "You got it, Mom," he said, and replaced himself with the ringtone distinctive to international calls.

"Good evening, this is Wheathaven," said Calvin Winslow.

Presently and despite the desiccation of her heart Ruth wished her friend the happiest of birthdays, and then, as though anyone in her family needed her, apologized that she could not speak longer and hung up.

IN LONELY MISCHIEF RUTH CUT FOUR CIRCLES OUT OF PAPER towel and placed them by the griddle. The children were still asleep and Alan, in the far corner of the living room, squinting at a slab of legal fiction under a single bulb. She ladled out four pancakes and pressed a circle into each, batter creeping across the apertures until the paper towels were absorbed. She ladled a fifth for herself.

Neither pancakes on a weekday nor their secret ingredient warranted comment from her family. Alan read his book at the table, Jamie and Rose feuded with melting candle wax, and Gretel was too young to disobey reality.

ANOTHER MORNING. ALAN TOOK A PHONE CALL, LEAVING RUTH to convey fried eggs and a full kettle to the breakfast table. She stepped on a horse chestnut—serially acquisitive, Jamie was that month hoarding toward arborism—and successfully metabolized her expletive. The children were silent in their warfare, at least. Her thigh was wet with tea.

Alan entered, preoccupied. "There's a Meeting at seven," he said. "Babies up." He surveyed the children. "Did you hear that, ladies and germs? No dillydallying."

"No pillypallying," said Jamie from behind his *D'Aulaire's*. Blithe Rose practiced cursive *c*'s on an old envelope; Gretel pretended to wash the plastic lids comprising her dishware for imaginary meals.

But in obedience, all Feders ate efficiently and arrived in the Meeting Hall, mid-flock, at 6:50. A weekday morning babies up

Meeting was rare; many heads were wet. They sang as they assembled, and sang because they assembled. The grown-ups knew to be uneasy. The Meeting Hall was muffled in damp white February air.

After "Jacob's Ladder," an elder stood and announced simply that Eddie and Tina Kupp had gone to the hospital late the night before, and that a baby had been born and called right back to God. They would be coming home from the hospital that afternoon. Rain began at the instant Ruth understood quite what the elder meant.

Danny Mueller volunteered the first line of "Ride On, King Jesus," and the Brotherhood swelled to join him. Monday's schedule was suspended, and a new rota of solemn tasks appeared on the bulletin board.

After taking the children to their groups, Ruth lay down in the lightly soiled mess of her marital bed and tried to decide if she felt anything.


EDDIE, TINA, AND BERYL RETURNED TO THE DORF SHORTLY after lunch. Ruth barely knew the Kupps, but had always admired in both an exhaustion she took for maturity. They had seemed sad even before losing Beryl, and now they formed the still center of a whirling, mourning community. Their return went fully observed but unannounced; their house had been cleaned, their cupboards stocked, their walls papered with a morning's drawings of angels and lambs from the Lower School.

After a private supper with the elders, Eddie and Tina presented Beryl at the evening Meeting. Families lined up to rotate slowly past the painterly tableau—Tina seated, cradling Beryl, Eddie at her shoulders, their other four children in meek array. The rain persisted. The Meeting Hall was grainy in the half light. Ruth dreaded approach, and distracted herself by trying and failing to identify the familiar smell coming from the kitchen. The line staggered forward by another family, and finally Ruth stood before Beryl; having spent the morning despairing at her own clinical regard for death, she was relieved to burst out sobbing when she finally saw the baby's perfect face and wine-black mouth.

Her garland was no bigger than a Ball jar lid, woven of baby's breath and roses from the picking garden. In the community, a woman had only three chances at adornment: her birthday, her own wedding, and May Day. Ruth realized it was Beryl's birthday. Rose commenced wailing as the line progressed, and Ruth's first worry was of melodrama.

After the presentation, Beryl was laid in a cradle in a room beside Eddie and Tina's. For every hour of the days before her burial, the community took shifts—an hour at a time, all through both nights—to sit with and sing to her. Young families were given the easiest waking hours, while Shalom sang in pairs until dawn.

And with dawn came the bus from Sugar Valley, bearing two dozen other brothers and sisters to take over a skeleton version of Twin Rivers work detail. As though on their own Dorf, they cooked supper, cleaned the common spaces, stoked the pellet stove, and watched the infants so that Twin Rivers might mourn purely. For the days leading up to the burial, children had no school but went to gather flowers and practice a song they had written for Beryl. Wednesday morning spat rain; all gathered indoors so that Eddie and Tina could hold their daughter for the last time, and then all proceeded outside, silently. Beryl was put in the earth, and the men of the community took turns helping to fill her grave.

Ruth cherished watching Alan when it was his turn at the spade, and took his hand walking back to the Dorf.

"What the elder said, in the morning Meeting," she began. She loved and wanted to communicate with every conceived soul. "He meant exactly what he meant."

Hers, language, was the cowardly euphemism. Real life was just a rough metaphor for God's plot. Alan let it be.

BARN RATS AFFLICTED KITTSON COUNTY, AND A BOUNTY WAS placed on their little skulls: for every rat killed or caught, Animal Control offered a dollar fifty. Jamie made nearly forty dollars before Bruno Dettweiler discovered his breeding operation behind the wood lot, and made him turn over the money to the Steward.

FOR THE BROTHERHOOD SO LOVED THE WORLD THAT IT SACRI-ficed sons by the Twin Cities–bound Greyhound-load. Community, the community said, was no protection against the temptations facing all of fallen creation; and yet the world was terrifying.

The sock story germinated in Sugar Valley and was global within the week; like a burr it clung to the beautiful news of Curtis and Annaliese Becker's engagement and rapid wedding. Ruth heard it first from Suzanne Stahl, a genius of misconstruction, and so thought little; but within the hour two other sisters had alluded to it in terms as alarming. An emergency Brotherhood was announced at snack.

Across the world, Dorfs crackled into the tie line. Each offered the others many many greetings, and Jörg invited Sugar Valley to explain their troubling discovery. Todd Braun, a minor Servant likely assigned to guide Sugar Valley's young people, could be heard accepting the microphone.

The day's rumors had at least been accurate to themselves; Todd braved his way through words the Brotherhood had designed an entire life to avoid. So little was known, so much feared; as Todd repeated the hideous term, every mind set to private definition, each projection a portrait of the projectionist. Hundreds of dirty films screened at once, to wincing. As in prayer, all eyes were cast down.

After Todd apologized his way into silence, Jörg spoke. It was in trials like these that the Lord worked through the Servants. Mildly, gently, Jörg challenged the community not to confront or punish their young people, but to show them more love. They prayed, sang, and disconnected from the tie line.

Rose and Gretel were long asleep by the time Alan and Ruth got home, but Jamie was up, crouched on a chair and squinting at an album of his own baby photos. His glasses lay folded among the ruins of an origami flock.

"My little Narcissus," she said, tucking in the tag of his T-shirt. He turned the page to admire his own first Christmas.

"Doesn't matter how good you look if you've got irreversible macular degeneration by the time you're twenty," Alan announced, his good-night. Ruth sat next down next to Jamie and joined him in wonder that a creature of his elfin precision first met the world as a fat-faced, snowsuited starfish.

"How was the Global?"

"It was a very serious Meeting. Opa reminded us that the only cure for sickness is love."

Jamie flipped to the end of the album. "Was there any food?"

"No," said Ruth. "It's bedtime."

Her son paused, jumped like a frog from his chair, and hopped into the hallway. Ruth went into the darkened girls' room. While her daughters panted softly, Ruth groped through Rose's sock drawer and pulled out two pairs of anklets, unworn. She withdrew.

Although he was already in bed, Alan's dim form seemed alert. "You doing okay, Mom?"

She left the socks on their dresser. She took off her watch. "Rose had two pairs but I don't think she's even worn them."

He spoke doubtlessly. "We don't need to worry about Rose."

But for hours and weeks later she could not, in empty moments, extract the phrase "sex socks" from her mind.

THE KITCHEN SISTERS WERE WINDSOCKS, EASILY AND OFTEN IN-spired. Preparing two meals for more than two hundred people was a thankless daily task, and their fantasy warranted; rare was the week when Stores did not brook a request for taco shells, or curry powder, or some other exotica requiring special order. They indulged the kitchen sisters as budgeting allowed.

Food was a deeply polarizing topic but one too low for regular Brotherhood discussion. Consequently did many break the Law of Roßdorf, questioning, among themselves, the spiritual health and intentions of kitchen sisters responsible for Swedish Seafood Casse-

role or Creamed Turkey Tacos. Crimes? The community was con-
stitutionally incapable of wasting food. The more challenging the
meal, the longer the community suffered its leftovers.

Under the direction of Elaine Wollmann, the kitchen attained
gross ambit. Elaine was the oldest of seven, the rest boys, the rest
married and fruitful while she remained single-hearted. The community sent her to a Swiss hospitality college in consolation, and
she returned a thirty-four-year-old woman on fire with gratitude.

Quickly the elders doubted the wisdom of their decision. Four
semesters in Bern had misinformed Elaine: she now expressed love
in napkin swans and inflatable desserts. The first meal she directed,
a Love Meal celebrating Johnny and Hedwig Wollmann's twentieth, cost and educated Stores dearly; the community proved hostile
toward Brie. At the end of the evening, twenty-three cheese plates
returned to the kitchen bearing twenty-three mauled rounds of
cheese, one scalped entirely.

Poor gourmet Elaine. She persevered, sure that brothers and sisters would come to appreciate dining as distinct from feeding. Certainly the kitchen sisters found her meal plans novel; none enjoyed
eating whitefish rillettes, but preparing them made for a jolly morning, and anything was more interesting than another dinner of
meatloaf, sauerkraut, and mash. And among the Brotherhood she
had allies: the Servant's wife, Barbar, who had eaten a real Sacher-
torte, could confirm the mastery of Elaine's, while known eccentric
Bruno Dettweiler defended her olive budget.

The elders were conflicted, and tried to solve the problem sideways. Stores was enlisted to force a famine on risky ingredients, but
Elaine improvised, hammering bacon into prosciutto and pickling

her own caper berries. Stores relented. Suffused with real vanilla, her *îles flottantes* baffled and sank.

In the end, only love could overcome love: the sudden death of Muriel Maerz left her widower, Peter, without companion and his six children motherless. In Elaine Wollmann he found an able wife and surrogate; she retired from the kitchen and served her new family humbly.

AFTER THE BLESSING AND ONE SONG, THE DOUBLE KITCHEN DOORS swung open and the Austeilers poured forth. Hot food was delivered in industrial metal bowls and sheet pans, cold food on melamine. The servers circulated constantly, in patterns as mysterious as the heavens, refilling emptied vessels or poaching food from table to table. Ruth wondered what primal capacity Austeiling expressed.

In middle age, Ruth made great demands of the younger Austeilers. She asked for her soup in an envelope, her ice cream on an Egyptian litter.

"Mom," said Alan, uncharmed.

ONE MORNING THE TABLE WAS SET ONLY FOR THREE.

"We're having a special breakfast," Ruth announced. She'd made cowboy coffee cake and let Gretel drink black tea out of a thimble. Ruth couldn't fathom giving the blessing, and so hastily depressed the toast lever after the morning song.

Rose and Gretel were cheerful in their morning duties, incurious to whatever had robbed the family of men. Ruth recalled childhood

in Edendale, when a neighbor's electrical fire had all the fathers out
at three in the morning, and hers came home sooty in the middle of
Sunday breakfast. It was the only time she had known him to sleep
in; when he reemerged for lunch, she was furious with revulsion.

Even then, she understood that terrible, important things happened in the night; night was a state of perpetual adult disaster, and
so she avoided it. She had also known that nothing was truly wrong
if her mother was still at home, plaiting her hair and humming the
St. Matthew's Passion. Ruth was no such ballast, but Rose was
anyway steady, and Gretel a good mimic.

Alan and Jamie were still missing at noon. Monday lunches
comprised whatever survived the kitchen's walk-in cooler over the
weekend, patched together with mayonnaise and supplemented
with pickles or slaw; that day it was bratwurst, cold pasta salad, rolls,
and apples for dessert. Rose gingerly deposited eleven macaroni elbows on her plate and covered them with ketchup. Ruth added a roll
without comment. When the meal closed, Rose returned to class
and forgot about everything that was not the Amazon rainforest.

For seven hours Ruth protected her daughters from panic. In
the eighth she broke, taking Rose from class and Gretel from her
play group and, in words of two syllables or less, explained that the
Kittson County sheriff had caught Jamie trying to hitchhike into
Winnipeg sometime after midnight.

THERE BEING NO DIRECT ROUTE, SPIRITUALLY, FROM A POLICE
station waiting room back to the embassy of God, Jamie was not
returned for two months. The Brothers had swift protocol for

disobedience like his, and a network of sufficiently God-fearing groups willing to shelter Dorf apostates.

"Did they send him to the Amish hog farm?" she asked her husband. They were in bed, the lights off, but from the rhythmic susurrations of his ankle stretches she knew he was awake. He had of late fallen prey to the charley horse.

Alan only grunted. He was in regular conference with the Brothers burdened with Jamie's para-Dorf preservation, but would tell her nothing about where and how their son was. This too was protocol; the community did not demand sanity from a mother in Ruth's position, but nor did they welcome catastrophe by trusting her.

"They wouldn't send him out West," she gambled. "Maybe one of those intentional communities? The one near St. Louis that does the nonviolence conference?"

His feet had ceased to swivel and he rolled onto his side, away from her. She pinched the back of his arm as hard as she could and then gave up until morning.

> *Hi Mom! Hi Rose and Gretel! Hi whichever dear Servant is reading this to make sure I'm not writing curse words!*
>
> *(In case you haven't heard already I'm at the L'Arche in St. Paul, which is mostly great. I do my own school stuff in the morning and then am with the residents after lunch: yarn crafts, library excursions, everyone buddy up, don't throw*

*your carrot sticks etc. There are ten adult residents and four*
*"volunteers" who care for them . . . as yet unclear whether I*
*am on the giving or receiving end of this care (but doesn't*
*Jesus basically say care is like a recycling symbol?) so I am just*
*doing what I'm told and going where I'm led and alerting all*
*present when I need to use the toilet in a public environment.)*

Jamie's only dispatch from exile arrived two days after he did. He appeared at lunch on Monday, wearing an oversize polo shirt she didn't recognize and talking faster than she could think; he talked all afternoon and then fell to twitchy sleep on the living-room sofa before dinner. By Wednesday he had forfeited the shirt and readjusted to community hours, though Ruth still found herself trying to impress him as though he were a guest.

It was after the Wednesday evening Meeting where Jamie narrowed his eyes and faked his own voice and asked the Brotherhood's forgiveness that Ruth read the entirety of his letter from the outside. He described the embarrassment of breakfast options one faced and the gentle pranks he plotted with his roommate, an older resident named Clive whose disability only occurred to Ruth the third time that Jamie called him "sweet."

There were arts programs and apprenticeships that Jamie had solicited for information, he wrote to her; he had borrowed a GED study guide from the library.

By the penultimate paragraph, his cursive had deteriorated into wavelets, and Ruth had to guess at several stretches of apparent confession. Maybe Jamie wrote that he faced simultaneous awareness and incomprehension of wanting a life that could not include her. Maybe he promised that he would see her again—a "somehow" was strikingly legible amid the scribble.

Her poor boy asleep in the next room, Ruth thought.


WHO WAS THE MYSTERIOUS CHARACTER OF LEG RUB?

Leg Rub had no body but many qualities: wit, acerbity, industry. Within one week, it took credit for four notes on the high school bulletin board, a postcard mailed from the neighboring postal code to Principal Bruno Dettweiler, and an unprintably demented letter to the editors of the student paper, *The Beehive*. Leg Rub was an aphorist, a critic, and a clown.

The high school were invited to confess responsibility, and parents exhorted to pray more adamantly against the spiritually vulnerable in their midst. Leg Rub went underground, but the Dorf still glittered with mischief. In Help Yourself, Anna McLeod discovered a single egg with "L. R." penciled onto one side.

At great psychic cost Ruth contained both the knowledge that only Jamie could be responsible and the conviction that he was not; she feared he would lie to her and so never asked, only smirking loyally when Leg Rub struck.


BERENICE DETTWEILER (NÉE DETTWEILER) APPROACHED DURING Shop Snack and wondered whether Ruth might take a walk with her. A year below Ruth in grade school, Berenice had leapfrogged, through marriage, into dominance. She had not, in the process, acquired a sense of humor, withstanding jokes as though suffering a fool. So armed, she won every conversation.

Ruth did not keep her wondering long, and Berenice returned the courtesy. She had come across Jamie in the act of writing a— here Berenice winced pityingly, for her faults, for her faults, for her most grievous faults—note on the high school bulletin board. Jamie had not fled, bless him, but neither had he seemed contrite.

Ruth only nodded, kicking her skirt forward, looking away from Berenice toward the Dorf perimeter. She would be obstinate in Jamie's stead, spare him the humiliation of a command disguised as dialogue.

Berenice spoke like a rod. "Bruno and I would like to bring this to the Servants."

That night, as the elder led the Brotherhood in holding Jamie to the light, Ruth struggled to create a face; from the inside, at least, none felt accurate to her confusion. She and Alan, sitting dumb as a dumpling beside her, had given each of these minds cause to judge and punish their child; and yet instead, each joined in the petition that Jamie's heart be truly won for Christ.

MIDMORNING, A NOTE APPEARED ON THE BULLETIN BOARD:

> *Will the dear high school boys who use the Swedish Hall for music practice kindly remember that wooden floors do not buff themselves?*

A second note in a different hand appeared after lunch:

*Dear is not a synonym for damn.*

It was quickly removed, and the relevant parties were encouraged to reflect on flippancy.

*Hazel Vale*

As garages existed to fix cars, and libraries to circulate books, the community existed as an embassy of Heaven on Earth; it was right there in the charter, after the First Law of Roßdorf and before the enumeration of martyred Anabaptists.

Ruth, out of character, had never doubted the sanity of such an ambition, and visiting a mortal embassy for a passport only strengthened the metaphor. Embassies were sanitary waiting rooms staffed by civil servants. Power was absolute but hidden in a back room, like some pulsing larval queen.

The young brother who met their now-diminished family at the Sudbury Airport held a sign he could not have made (colored-pencil daffodils for brackets; "Welcome, dear Feders!") and drove them westward into the woods of Ontario with such palpable devotion to the task that even Ruth knew not to tamper with his concentration. He dropped them off in front of the Meeting Hall, then continued on to deliver their luggage. Ruth, Alan, and Gretel were left to face the inevitable salvo of greetings.

RUTH THOUGHT OF THE COMMUNITY'S CHARTER MISSION AS SHE entered Hazel Vale's Meeting Hall for the first time.

It was hundreds of miles from Edendale and Gracefield, and peopled with strangers all the stranger for shared expatriation. Yet Ruth knew she was safe—immune as a diplomat—on gleaming linoleum, fragrant with the same liquid soap she could only smell clearly at the moment of arrival.

CERTAIN ITEMS OF CHOCOLATE HAD BEEN IN CIRCULATION FOR years. Ruth had twice received the same Mozart-themed nougat bonbon from people on two different Dorfs; she knew because the first time, she had carefully unfoiled it and scratched her initials in the bottom. On second circuit she gave it to Arden Ayler, the six-year-old downstairs, who discovered it had long gone rancid but made a point of eating it anyway. Either humility or insanity propelled a community in which only children felt entitled to eat their own candy.

ON MOTHER'S DAY ALL QUALIFYING SISTERS WERE BUSED TO Ramsey Lake with assurances that the Dorf would cope without them until supper. Ruth only minced in the shallows for a few minutes before joining the Omas on a shaded tarp. Suzanne Stahl, who loved the water, hoisted up her skirt and slip and rushed into the water like a stung hen.

In the shadow of Karin Knultz's wheelchair, Ruth listened to an aimless discussion of geranium care. She had grown up across the hall from the Knultzes and still tensed reflexively around Karin, who had been swift and humorless and admonishing. Now dementia had rendered her docile. She slept, crumpling sideways in her wheelchair, eyelids fluttering behind a new pair of eyeglasses that became sunglasses in bright light.

ALAN'S PASSION FOR AMERICAN SIGN LANGUAGE (ASL) WAS quickly subsumed by a derivative passion for describing American Sign Language (ASL). His was a limited reservoir of anecdotes, and actually seemed to shrink as his proficiency grew. Superlatives he explained with the signs for beard, big beard, and biggest beard, the last of which required a mortifying flourish of pursed fingers. Stories told in the present tense he tossed over his shoulder to back-date. His demonstrations numbed Ruth; disassociating from her own body seemed the only way to disassociate from his.

She felt the same flinching hatred for the flesh whenever he drank from a long-necked beer bottle or snored. She wished for a ray gun that shot beams of humiliation.

VISITORS WERE A THREEFOLD BLESSING. TO HOST AN OUTSIDER provided the entertainment of the outsider himself, the performance of roaming the Dorf with a new character, and the excuse to request double coffee and biscuits from Stores. Ruth was fiercely proprietary of her guests, but, as with her books and her internet access, knew that she might be asked to give them up at a moment's notice without explanation.

So it was with Marion Morris, an extremely vertical woman inclined toward communal living, fermented foods, and other vaunted, boring Goods. She came for supper one Saturday and was assigned to the Feders, possibly in compensatory blessing for Jamie's absence. Ruth found the assumption of transitivity insulting, in the flesh.

Though usually pronged with curiosity, she was passive with this guest, and only observed as Alan deployed his favorite questions.

In her civilian life, Marion toiled at something lamentably bureaucratic—Ruth could not summon care here, but merely placed their guest in mental fluorescents and thought elsewhere. She lived in a vaguely intentional community two towns over from Hazel Vale. Not a full community of Goods, and without common work, but cooperative and politically protein deficient; just enough like the Brotherhood to be nothing like it. A garden plot, yes, but Marion had gone alone to Thailand, Hungary, Morocco, without steward or the Steward's pouch of money; after supper she would bicycle home, out from under the Brotherhood's loving net.

At thirty-eight, Marion was ten years younger than Ruth. She was unmarried and fell into handsome lines when quiet. At dinner Alan concluded his routine on American Sign Language.

Did Marion struggle with living in community? Ruth asked with private spade-shaped malice; the Brotherhood might be torturous but at least it was a right and internally coherent torture. She wanted Marion to complain of fractious disputes of faith, property, and purpose; to acknowledge that Ruth's was the righter way.

But Marion sprung affable, quoting Dorothy Day, sympathetic rather than admiring. In spite of everything that had been taken from her, or never granted to begin with, Ruth had always held a monopoly on brainy female despair. The community offered no competition; her rivals were Weil, Day, Flannery O'Connor, all rendered unthreatening by celebrity. They would never sit in the home she shared with Alan, reflect with her precision and wit, prove Ruth the black mirror. The imp of ungenerosity came, scampering up her spine.

"We forget how lucky we are to have the support of brothers and sisters," she said, eyes wifely at Alan. "There are so many forces working against true marriage and the family." She knew not what she spoke except that it was politic; yet Marion would not cower.

"I have a hard enough time living with my own mind," said Marion, now at Alan. "I can't imagine how challenging marriage must be."

Marion returned to Hazel Vale for another visit three weeks later, and was given to the Curtis and Annaliese Beckers to play with. From across the dining hall, Ruth watched them treat her gently.

RUTH WAS RELEASED INTO THE NEIGHBORHOOD TO MAKE HUMAN connections. Every other Saturday afternoon she visited with Merle, a beaky and fretful widow living down the lane. Their visits quickly assumed a formality that left no room for affection: Ruth arrived at three, bearing one loaf of fresh bread and one jar of whatever jam was in the Help Yourself room. Merle made a performance of veiling the loaf under a tea towel on the kitchen counter, where it would hide for the duration of the visit; to Ruth, she gave snack cakes and a can of soda to bring back for Gretel.

Then, for seventy-five minutes, the two women would talk about such things as popular books and terrible news from foreign countries.

Merle had actually traveled to South Africa with her late husband, Roland, she revealed repeatedly.

Brooding on the living-room floor after one such visit, Ruth realized that she did not like Merle. She shared this with Alan, who was reading a book about Nazis in the next room, but he was either shocked into silence or did not hear her.

RUTH WAS ALARMED TO FIND AN INFLATABLE PUMPKIN ON MERLE'S porch. She couldn't think what would possess anyone, let alone a Christian, to buy such an odd thing. It was perfectly cube shaped.

Merle made no mention of the decoration that afternoon, but did wonder whether the community would be sending trick-or-treaters into the neighborhood that year.

"Oh, we don't like to scare the children," Ruth said, thinking of the square pumpkin. "But we will be celebrating the harvest." She described the mulled cider and wending lantern parade, and discovered herself a persuasive proponent of an event that had only ever inspired her to migraine. "The children just love to get into the fall spirit," she concluded, mildly aghast at herself.

Merle, who had not been listening, nodded anxiously. They were silent, and then, for the second time that afternoon, Merle asked Ruth if she had heard of Mitch Albom. Ruth still had.

ALAN HAD THE BROTHERHOOD THAT DAY, AND WAS SCHEDULED to read a Simone Weil quote that Ruth copied out for him over breakfast.

Between the hours of four and six she'd lain awake thrumming with excitement. It was a provocation, the Weil, and bound to cause argument. She scripted the freewheeling debate in her head, and was thrilled and nervous at what she imagined herself saying.

Tobias took Alan aside before the Brotherhood. Ruth saved him a seat, stinking with anticipation. But when he stood, it was not to speak of the tendency toward fascism that slept in every Christian's heart, but to announce that Brother Edmund Dampf in Edendale had been called to God suddenly in the night.

All one hundred seventy-four members began to sing "There Is a Balm in Gilead." Edmund Dampf had been restless, living for years in acrimony outside the community, and they thanked God that he was home when he entered the Upper Church.

Alan closed the Meeting, and the adults streamed into the sunshine for the traditional Sunday hike.

Gretel had invited herself along on another family's excursion, so Alan and Ruth did one loop around the Meeting Hall and then returned to their living room for the remainder of the day.

EACH DORF HAD A SPECIALTY. CEDAR HOLLOW TAPPED MAPLE syrup. Twin Rivers grew blueberries. Gracefield's butchery turned out reels of venison sausage. Two clever brothers in Edendale brewed beer.

Bought products were subject to regional fetishism. The English communities had Marmite and treacle, but no peanut butter; the Americans had superior coffee creamer and inferior tea. Canada's only advantage was the Coffee Crisp, which Ruth eschewed in stubborn loyalty to a claim she'd once made about the worthless-ness of wafers. Visitors were expected to weight their suitcases with groceries, since it all tasted at least twice as good when a brother or sister carried it on their person.

Free trade was not without risks. Teenage Silas Stahl spent four hours in Frankfurt's immigration holding after a Ziploc bag of cit-ric acid powder, essential for lemon pies but unavailable in En-gland, exploded in his carry-on before he could deliver it to his aunt.

Now Ruth distressed the sewing sisters. She did not want a new dress; she had three, wore one, and resented even that. Her best dress was a dark purple and gray stripe that pardoned dirt and was washed only at Gretel's intervention. The other two were plaids, one green and one navy, and both made her feel like a piece of patio furniture.

Edeltraud Ayler, a straight-speaking mother of eight, ran the sewing room. For brothers she made clothing, but for sisters she prescribed it. Vanity could be curbed with a busy print. Meekness might be rewarded with a rare Tyrolean blue. Because a sister risked admonishment the instant she mistook her appearance for her self, many feigned indifference about dress assignment. There were al-ways vaguely naked people in the Third World to be glad one wasn't. Anyhow, in a community of goods they were only ever tem-porary stewards of even their best dresses. Clothing, like flesh, ought be maintained with respect and detachment.

Ruth detached with ease; her life was one long, loud Velcro re-lease from the world. But to pretend to respect her dresses would be to lie. To wash them before they were filthy, to iron them on Saturday night and arrive at Family Meeting creaseless as though God minded would be to lie. All of this she planned to explain to Edeltraud, who had threatened jokingly to steal and bury her dress.

But when a fresh bundle appeared on her laundry shelf, Ruth was chastened with gratitude: the sewing sisters had merely, kindly duplicated her best dress. Now she could go twice as long disguised as a human.

In 2003, Merlin Klee died and Ruth stopped sending Dorothy Mueller (long a Wollmann) the annual postcard with "That'll do" printed calmly, unsigned.

For the usual failure of reasons, Ruth awoke miserable. Alan snored. She prayed for her children, for strength to cope with the day, for relief from her anger. She put on her housecoat and mobcap.

She asked and was granted forgiveness for her sins, knowing full well that she would sin again immediately. The living room was lit, the breakfast table set, and Carol sat tatting, squeaking on the Naugahyde sofa cushion.

"Good morning, Carol."

Their new Shalom girl was freshly imported from Gracefield. Carol, who could tat without watching her hands, beamed at Ruth. "It's just a marvelous day today."

Ruth found the remark implausible and went to shower.

The table had acquired eggs and bread when she returned. Gretel, half her head braided, was cross-legged on the floor tracing a portrait of Tupac Shakur that Ruth had printed for her earlier in the week. Alan emerged from the bedroom with a stack of books: the Bible, selected writings of Blumhardt father and son, and two copies of John Grisham's *The Firm*, one in French, from which he was attempting to extract fluency. He had announced the project over a year ago and made steady regress since; still, the books followed him from room to room.

"Grendel," he said, seating himself, "breakfast."

Gretel did not look up from her drawing. "But Carol's not here."

But she was, then, a swan of efficiency with a French press in one hand and a cozied kettle in the other. "Good morning, Alan."

Alan nodded. The beverages landed. Gretel stood but did not come to the table; she slouched against the windowsill, scowling and finishing her braid.

They sang, Alan read a bracing Blumhardt quote, and the meal began in blessed quiet. Ruth was already ready for the day to end, but Carol would not be discouraged. "I was out for a walk this morning and the sunrise was just marvelous."

"Wow, Carol." Gretel spiked an egg. "That sounds marvelous."

"Grendel, enough," said Alan.


THE HIGH SCHOOL'S PRODUCTION OF *PEER GYNT* PROVIDED RUTH with one reliable joke.

The production itself was an aberration. In the community, theater and lying were squares and rectangles. Though a muslin-shrouded Shalom reenacted parables on occasion, the high school students were discouraged from acting. Like sports, theater tainted the air with competition, and there was little that killed the child-like spirit faster than performance.

Yet in late fall, Curtis Becker had announced that the high school would perform *Peer Gynt*, and that the cast list was already on the bulletin board, sparing everyone the sins attendant to the audition process. High school hearts shredded with anxiety while Curtis went on to discuss a field trip to Science North.

News of the play wicked through the Dorf. Kyle Hauptmann was cast as Peer Gynt.

Kyle was the last remaining Hauptmann boy in Hazel Vale, from a family once known for its density of Hauptmann boys. Their father, Marcus, a mason and plumber, seemed so purely masculine that he could have no more contributed to the creation of a girl than he could a porpoise. His tiny wife, Morina, bore seven boys, and when all seven were at home, needed two trolleys to convey their food from family supper pickup. Ruth suspended them in memory from afar one Sunday afternoon. They had returned from trapping, the boys in single file behind Marcus, each swinging a limp hare in each hand.

Ruth addressed all boys between the ages of six and sixteen by any name she felt like. This was funny, and moreover, in that bracket boys were only test souls, no more or less individuated for being called Douglas or Jason. The Hauptmanns begged athletic, monosyllabic names; they passed for Sams and Robs, whoever they were. All seven ate well of the community's Stores, grew tall and noble in their father's outline, and, beginning with Jack in 2002, left the Dorf without compunction.

One after the other they declined baptism, regrouping in the world and working, all of them, for a boutique contractor in neighboring Chelmsford. It was worse that they left without acrimony and visited without suffering; perhaps God really had called them to the world of printed T-shirts and cohabitation before marriage. Although Marcus and Morina rarely discussed it, their absent boys were a shame and a failure.

Only Kyle remained, though his voice had dropped from the community's prayers and songs. At seventeen, he brooked few adjectives. He worked, he Austeiled, he maintained a modest curiosity in robotics. The community grieved as his soul dwindled in that teenage way, and so they gave him Peer Gynt.

Kyle's class schedule was halved to accommodate rehearsal. Every afternoon he paced the Cow Loop and practiced his lines. Morina skipped Shop Snack to bring him cocoa and confirm that he wouldn't rather come inside, frost considered. The community grew expectant. A week before the first show, Kyle appeared at Saturday supper with hair bleached blond, the better to play a Norwegian wastrel.

Ruth's imp awoke. "You should do that," she told Gretel. "You would look like a dandelion."

"I would look like a freak," Gretel said, looking at herself in the back of a spoon. Alan, who had caught only the end of the exchange, raised one eyebrow at Ruth but remained silent, as the Austeilers commenced circulation with chafing dishes of roast chicken.

Having married into the middle third of the alphabet, Ruth was invited to see the second performance of *Peer Gynt*. For months the community prepared for a play that, by expert account, compounded symbolism on symbolism and meant everything at once. After the third of Curtis Becker's talks, delivered over lunch and this time parsing Ibsen's political allegory, Carol succumbed to her own imp and confessed to the Shop sisters that the whole production seemed a bit high-minded. "You know there are some people who just can't take things for what they are. I always say, a rose is a rose is a rose." Ruth unfocused her eyes and nodded slowly as Carol elaborated into nonsense.

The curtain finally rose on a stage empty but for what looked like a gigantic doghouse.

"Peer Snoopy," Ruth whispered to Alan, who ignored her.

But she deployed the joke repeatedly, twice to Silas Stahl, who each time giggled nervously at Ruth's deranged little lie.

To autoplagiarize—how would Christ construe this as sin, and how could she not? A murderer could not feel worse than Ruth, exposed in laziness of thought.

That Silas was only a Shalom boy and duty bound to indulge her was no comfort. She avoided him for weeks.


"So I should pick up the laundry today or what," said Alan, running his knife between thumb and forefinger to collect the last streak of jam. Ruth tilted her head, malice on a stalk.

Every time Alan ended a statement with "or what," Ruth loathed him acutely. It meant nothing, she struggled to explain; or it was worse, a dead stump of curiosity where another sentence could have grown. He was not the only offender. "Or what" was a new affliction on the Dorf. Ruth no sooner hated it from Alan than she began saying it herself, to his maddening glee.

"The Meeting today is high school up, or what," she said carelessly one morning. Alan expelled a single vindictive snort.

"Your mother," he announced to Gretel, "contains multitudes."

"My name is Legion," Ruth said eventually, pride restored.

The plague of or-whatism inspired Tobias to admonish the Brotherhood for empty speech, which was second only to religious speech in friendship with sin. Tobias's voice tolled like a heavy bell, or whatever medieval technology—Ruth was dim on the Dark Ages—signaled danger from afar.

All were encouraged to regroup after the Meeting to reflect on their failures. Classically, the Feders joined the Kessler household for *Wohngemeinschaft*, where Alan inflated before the tripled audience and said the same things but more so. Ruth could not believe that Timo and Petra followed his bluster, but nor could she believe that it pained them; they were natural Christians in their suffering of fools.

While Alan held forth, Timo worked at his cobbling. Ruth recalled his arrival in Edendale in 1991, more than twenty years ago, from a food cooperative in Cologne imploding for lack of commitment to Christ. The Dorf was crowded back then—between construction and new life they spared no beds—but Timo cheerfully threw his knapsack up into a hayloft and slept there until well into his novitiate.

Built like a cricket, he wore women's jeans and aviator glasses, but made both look more frugal than eccentric. It was Timo who relieved Ruth of her misapprehension about bell-bottoms, and so kindly: he had not even laughed when explaining that the bells were at the bottom, not on them.

"You know what word we use too much?" Alan asked. Ruth's life was the silent composition of such a list.

"*Interesting*," he continued. "If you believe the high schoolers, everything they don't like and don't want to think about is interesting."

Ruth's sighs were the whetstone against which he sharpened his arguments.

"London was interesting. The homeless people were interesting. I bet if we banned interesting we'd have a bunch of mutes on our hands."

Ruth felt the fissure of good and evil run straight through her heart. Why did he repeat these performances? Why wasn't he ashamed?

Alan continued, untrammeled. "That would be pretty interesting, huh, Mom."

When Timo had asked for baptism, the community had worried only that he would struggle to articulate in words a faith gracefully evident in action. His English was worse than his German, itself inferior to his handiwork; compared even to brothers from the Colonies, Timo demonstrated material genius. He fit the world like a jigsaw puzzle, laying tile, deftly thumping faulty boilers back into action, and cobbling leather shoes for anyone who asked.

The combination of his good nature and crickety bearing rendered Timo sexless, which pleased the elders. So many young people, their own included, sought marriage as salvation; Timo seemed oblivious. Many sisters requested him. After baptism he had been counseled to contact Petra Braun, then the Laundry Mama in

Wheathaven, and with characteristic, childlike trust, he wrote to her, offering his thoughts on the Lord's Prayer. Next to his loopy signature he drew himself, in lederhosen and knapsack, scaling a gigantic boot and emitting musical notes.

They'd wed within three months, and Petra bore Matti within the year. They seemed, to Ruth, a faultless couple. She never heard them speak to one another in public, let alone quarrel.

Matti quickly received siblings of Martina, Melitte, and Meike, and all four joined their father in cobbling. Soon the whole Dorf was shod in one of three styles: slip-on loafers, lace-up work boots, or brogues, made from oddments bought cheap from a tannery in Mattawa. A boot-shaped sign converted the old chicken coop into a shoe shop.

Petra had the prow and freckling shared by all the Brauns, a prolific Swiss family descended from one of the community's few villains. As a Servant, Ulli Braun had sought his own glory through manipulation, separating husbands from wives and expelling several from the community entirely. Ruth had viewed him only once, long after his exclusion, repentance, and readmission to the Brotherhood. He had lain in a coffin, waxen and bright. Although the community published an account of his sins, Ulli's children and grandchildren were carefully spared. Sin was not congenital, and Petra was allowed to marry Timo.

There were so many biblical invectives to live as little creatures, to turn and sleep like dogs in God's grace. Timo and Petra had some of that; they tended one another gently, did the tasks that needed them, and took Alan's pause in monologue to suggest that the four of them might sing a few evening songs before retiring.

RUTH AND ALAN WERE SENT ON A MIDLIFE COMMISSION TO A Fulfillment Logistics conference in Barrie. For four days and three nights, not a blink in God's time, they would be off the Dorf. Though Alan had known of the trip months in advance, Ruth had been protected from anticipation, and learned only the morning of departure when she was sulking at her eggs.

"Cheer up, Mom," Alan said. The frequency of the statement had mitigated the radical vacuity of its content. Ruth glowered out at the dark morning, hoping bedward, wishing Gretel would leave for school and Carol vaporize.

"I picked up the laundry this morning."

Simone Weil had written something about destroying happiness in others—that it was as grave a crime as destroying the finest art. It must be true, happiness being so improbably intricate, and Ruth did flinch to imagine dragging a paring knife through *Water Lilies*.

"Earth to Mom."

She looked at Alan with emptied eyes. "Space travel is a hoax," Ruth said.

"I picked up the laundry this morning because we're going to Barrie after the Meeting."

The future resumed!

"What has Barrie done to deserve us?"

Alan contained a belch; he had lately developed reflux. "Conference, nerd stuff. The internet said we should be there in time for the luncheon, but you should bring something to eat in the car."

"Luncheon?" Gretel's sarcasm was aimless.

"It's three letters beyond lunch and you're not invited." Ruth turned with charity to her Shalom girl, but Carol's complicity flashed as brazen as young flesh.

"I prepared a cooler for you last night," the girl said.

Ruth was blessed with no desire to destroy Carol's happiness.

SUMMARIZING A *PSYCHOLOGY TODAY* ARTICLE HE HAD HEARD SUMmarized on the radio, Alan toured the car park twice and selected a spot psychologically proven to deter theft. He locked and unlocked and relocked the car, perambulated once to scan for dings, and declared himself satisfied.

Ruth reflected on cosmetics as she approached the front desk of the Barrie Holiday Inn, where a pair of fringed bovine eyes opened and closed at her. Makeup allowed one to lie without speaking. The concierge asked if they'd had a pleasant journey.

Ruth knew Alan's approach by the rhythmic malfunction of their rolling suitcase on the marble, and smiled at the eyes, named Angela, which opened and closed again. She moved to stand behind her husband as he perplexed Angela with his thoughts on parking psychology. They arrived well before the luncheon, a cold buffet that caused Ruth to become insane. It activated the only animal instincts she possessed; she became a starving marsupial in the wild, filling her pockets with fistfuls of rare snacks. Panic and thrill and madness at once; Alan, as though the world were not a scarce hell, watched faces instead of plates. He loitered by a bank of carafes and fed himself cherry tomatoes from one cupped hand, waiting for encounters. Ruth secreted nearly a pound of cold cuts before conceding to join him.

"I'm sure I'm the only wife in attendance," she said. Neither death nor conventions interrupted the eternal bondage of matrimony. Since marriage, they had shared a bed every night but for those when she was recuperating in the Motherhouse; the community could not afford name-brand toothpaste, but had from the first year of its profitability paid to gird married brothers from loneliness in hotels.

"Do you want to go back up to the room?" Alan asked.

Without him, Ruth realized he meant, and realized that she did, if only to empty her laden pockets. Alan gave her one of their two key cards and asked that she deadbolt the door.

She looked back on her way out and caught him loitering at the edge of a conversation between two men in blazers. Ruth felt a glitch of sympathy for her husband.

WHILE ALAN CIRCULATED AROUND FOLDING TABLES, RUTH commenced investigation. The Barrie Holiday Inn was a puzzle of false bottoms and hollow walls, and mostly empty moreover. She prowled the halls and plumbed the basement for nearly an hour before risking surveillance, and even then it was just a vested teenager smoking in the laundry. Still, she backed up slowly, both hands at her purse.

This was the world she wanted, and wanted to escape: a maze with strangers, and somewhere within it a single room containing the man who bored her.

LOIS LOMAX, A CONVICTED PACIFIST AND CELIBATE, JOINED THE community at twenty-eight and immediately descended into multiple sclerosis. She trembled and soiled herself; her mind flickered, then failed. This made her no less a blessing, all knew to say, and Ruth suspected it was true. In her illness, Lois, though once magnetic, could tempt no one.

Her care was divided among three Shalom girls in eight-hour shifts. Martina Kessler bathed and toileted in the morning, then escorted Lois to the Shop for recreational labor; mild Virginia Kupp took over at lunch. And Adelheid Wollmann, in whom the community saw both talent and arrogance, slept on a cot beside Lois at night, a task that afforded no scope (or audience) for precocity.

Defending Lois's body from itself was one challenge, and her mind from the Devil another. She spoke in tongues when confused, and once bit Martina during a sponge bath. So had the early Christians spoken in tongues, Ruth thought, unable to parse the metaphor, dubious of the lot. They grasped snakes and babbled and taught her nothing about mercy.

Mostly and shamefully it was that she envied Lois. Before the illness, Ruth had admired Lois's self-possession, the confidence with which she rejected her life in the world, her braying laughter. After, she simply envied her the immunity bestowed by the disease. The Brotherhood banned anger at Lois, even when she interrupted a Meeting to confess to an abortion, even when she shrieked during the Lord's Prayer.

Children unafraid of Lois loved her to the point of trouble. They baited her and encouraged naughtiness; Ruth had never despised a child more than when she caught a minor Mueller, well aware at eleven years old, asking Lois for an explanation of sex.

Five years into her sisterhood and opaque with the disease, Lois was disappeared. She was farewelled with no Love Meal or hand-shaking, and even her special utensils were left in the kitchen of the Carriage House, ergonomic.

Rapid ferreting informed the curious that Lois's parents had demanded her return—had been demanding it for years, went insinuation—finally threatening the community with a lawsuit that could not be prayed away. Carol, font of speculation, imagined Lois straitjacketed and in prison. This vision did not perturb Ruth, al-though like everyone else she became defensive at the family's accusations of brainwashing.

RUTH HAD A FRIEND IN BROTHER OH. HE CAME TO THE COMMU-nity on his own, from South Korea, by channels unknown to even the eldest of the elders; he arrived without property or debt. For months he joined them in work and Meetings but would or could not speak.

Brother Oh revived Ruth's childhood theory that all minds op-erated in English, but needed internal translation to speak. He wasn't an idiot, although he had a pervert's Adam's apple and nod-ded constantly. "Our Brother of perpetual affirmation," Ruth called him. Brother Oh's compliance outpaced his need for language, and he was categorically admired in silence.

All of Brother Oh's evidence fit into the single accordion file he brought to Ruth at Shop Snack. He delivered it with two hands and looked away as she unpacked it onto her lap: a sheaf of sheer Korean documents and a small album of gold-embossed, dove-gray cardstock.

Brother Oh hummed idly, agitating one knee, while Ruth looked at his photographs. The first was his parents' wedding photo, expressing all the joy of a full-body double mugshot. In the second, the couple was joined by the infant Oh, who sat expressionless as a cushion on his mother's lap. One cheek was grossly swollen and bandaged. In the third picture, his army headshot, he looked newer to the world than a child.

Ruth found herself disturbed by the photograph of Brother Oh as a baby. The lump and bandage suggested not sickness but freakishness, the kind of disability with which God teaches parents how He feels about man; they heard this every time one died. Over the decades, a number of babies born to the community had proven incompatible with life, and each had tested the community's capacity for euphemism. One had a wet crater where his jaw was meant to be. Another, encephalitic, lacked a skull. At every burial God was thanked for fulfilling his own definition through the incomprehensible giving and taking of souls. Forced ponderance of eternity was a gift.

But Brother Oh had not died. Moreover, his current face betrayed nothing of the Lord's metaphor.

Ruth entreated explanation, but his pantomimes were interrupted by the snack bell. That afternoon, she made the same typing error three times in preoccupation with Brother Oh's vanished lump.

FOUR YEARS LATER, THE COMMUNITY WON ITS NEXT KOREAN speakers, a bumptious family of Kims with great faith and a seven-year-old with Down syndrome. Ruth had never dammed her wonder at Brother Oh's childhood, and now, finally, could broker a translation through the Kim family: his parents had taped a Ping-Pong ball to his cheek.

Kyongguk Kim had practiced law in Seoul before lofting his family into the Brotherhood, and spoke of crime in the neutral terms of contractual failure. Evenly he explained: a Ping-Pong ball deterred an obdurate child from sleeping face down lest he deform his skull in preference for one cheek. Kyongguk looked again at the infant Oh on his parents' lap. "In Korea, everyone wants to look the same."

"I can't imagine," said Ruth, taking back the photograph.

FOR THEIR TWENTY-FIRST WEDDING ANNIVERSARY, ALAN AND Ruth went to Sudbury for three hours. The Steward provided car keys and a pleather envelope of three $20 notes. Alan carried the envelope in his otherwise empty backpack, and Ruth could not explain why its deflated form made her furious.

He drove carefully while reciting his now-enshrined anecdotes about road fatalities. When she turned on the radio, he mildly turned it off and kept talking. His immunity to her anger only enraged her further.

Every passing car was an opportunity to project pathos; she

made eye contact and tried to look like a woman abducted. She interrupted Alan's defense of defensive driving to ask whether he would mind if she opened the door and jumped out into traffic.

"Not funny, Mom," he said, eyeing the rearview mirror. But he was quiet until parking moved him to mutter.

HE WANTED BEER AND SAUSAGE, AND SHE WANTED TO WINDOW-shop. As Christ was the leading head of the church's body, so did the husband coordinate the parts of his family, and Alan led his to food and drink. Zum Zeiss Beer Hall smelled of a burp and fulfilled his desire; Ruth requested only a coffee. The neon clock above the bar grew slower and more lurid the more she loathed, until her impatience stopped time altogether.

At time's end Alan examined the check, explained to her his gratuity rationale, and broke one bill of the community's money. She would have forfeited all civilization to be alone then; her coffee cost an improbable five dollars.

To the Dollar Mall. Alan preferred to wait outside, and Ruth preferred him there too, so they agreed to meet at the car. Every aisle arrested her. She wanted crinkling double-decker sponges and foot-shaped flyswatters, plastic flowers, plastic multipurpose hooks; she filled her basket with treasure and then left it on an empty shelf and filled another. She concluded in the beauty aisle, and there sniffed methodically every lotion, shampoo, and deodorant. Each predicted a soul's worth of experiences; her favorite was a synthetic gardenia hair rinse in a tapered lavender bottle, and against all covenants Alan appeared near the checkout, willing to buy it for her.

JÖRG, IN ORBIT AND ON LOAN FROM EDENDALE, LED THE MEETING that Sunday morning, on the patio in the rain.

"All glory be to God on this beautiful day!" he said.

They sang some morning songs, and some rainy day songs, and one entreating the jolly old sun to show his face. The kids went off to their groups just as the rain abated; Gretel kept her raincoat hood up and scowled when Ruth politely advised that she stop showing off.

The Meeting resumed. Jörg had been thinking, he revealed, and as evidence had a new challenge for the Brotherhood. "Too much, we are buzzing around like bees, thinking God just wants us to be busy. But when we are always working working working, we are actually keeping God out of our hearts. We need sometimes for silence, and white space, to listen for His message."

The community was to spend the afternoon seeking white space. Ruth sought and found it easily, back in bed with a bland novel about an Australian veterinarian. She was, however, not surprised when at dinner that evening several at their table confessed to industry.

"I just knew," said Edeltraud Ayler, "that if I didn't get the buffing done today I'd have that imp on my shoulder all week."


ONE AFTERNOON, RUTH FOUND ON THE UNIVERSITY OF NEW Mexico's website a photograph of a man who could only be her brother. She had dared search his name while Alan was occupied with a conference call about labeling rubrics. He spoke drolly into his headset while doing the daily leg stretches that comprised his new health regimen. James, now a professor of environmental science and wearer of ties, looked kind and tired in his faculty portrait, as though he had just received a poor but predictable prognosis for a beloved dog. She could not parse his brief biography, which omitted mention of God, community, joy, and regret; it was merely a string of affiliations and Latin words. *James Scholl went shoeless for his fifteenth year to prove a point about self-discipline,* she would have added to his biography. *James Scholl once got a concussion falling from an orange crate balanced on the back of a fat old draft horse named Pongo.*

She imagined sending him an email, but instead prayed that he might think of her right then and absorb in one instant the sum of her life since he'd left. As for him, he'd marched straight off the pages of history. Though she suspected he'd written after he left, no letters arrived, and by the time she thought to look, his details had been scrubbed from the community's birthday book.

The first Brotherhood she ever attended spun round James's absence. Nauseated, Ruth doubted her parents when they professed ignorance before the community. In the low-lit Meeting Hall, among men and women suddenly raw with conviction, she watched her father lie.

Esther stood beside him, her eyes nowhere. They held hands while he spoke, but when it ended they returned to their living room and resumed dull parenthood. He set the table for breakfast, she added a few blocks to the perpetual afghan project that lurked in a wicker basket beneath the sofa. Neither sitting nor standing cured Ruth's panic. She did not know where to lodge her alarm, and finally went to the boys' room. She sat on the lower bunk, already stripped and squeaky, and waited for Jeremiah's acknowledgment.

Above her, he cleared his throat and turned a page. It was a Tolkien book in such high demand that the library maintained a waiting list, and James had waited nearly three weeks for his turn. Just the day before he'd kept it on his lap through breakfast and tormented Jeremiah, who was much lower on the list and defenseless against plot revelation.

"I bet they'll let you keep it until the due date," she said to the top bunk. "At least he didn't take it with him."

At the Meeting, Jeremiah had sat not with their family but in a hedge of high school boys at the perimeter, his face as vacant as Esther's. Perhaps he too had known. Four-year-old Sue Ellen, already several hours into an untroubled sleep, certainly hadn't; she wept theatrically at the news, fled the breakfast table, and was shortly heard playing hospital with Annaliese Ayler in the corridor.

Now Jeremiah remained silent. She was enervated with hatred for her family, James most of all. It was as though he had rejected the laws of gravity. What could make sense if not the Brotherhood of all men? What, now, would he obey? Idly Ruth wondered why atheists even bothered with the conventions of spelling and grammar.

The bunk squealed above her, and Jeremiah's feet dangled at eye level. "I hope he gets shot and killed and feels like a moron."

The next morning, she noticed the Tolkien sodden and face down on the bathroom floor. James had ripped the last chapters from the binding before he'd left.

Time had leached her memories of feeling. What anger she felt she felt toward herself, and by extension Alan, though without the delusion of authority. She now knew her anger to be a form of stupidity.

Ruth drafted an email to her brother to this effect, a dense, puzzling paragraph that only made sense when read headlong. She did not burden him with questions, for the idea of prolonged correspondence bored her from the horizon; hers was a singular transmission, meant to remind him that her mind remained, and he was on it. In the postscript, she explained that the attached image of her family was several years outdated, and that but for the white hen, incongruous but not unhappy on Jamie's lap, all members remained alive.

There was distraction in Alan's voice, Ruth noticed; his conference call began the wheeling descent into farewells. She sent the email and sped to her outbox, where she reread it and realized she'd never attached the picture.

THERE WERE YEARS OF CHILDHOOD DURING WHICH MORE THAN half of the Brotherhood had been in exclusion. She recalled periods of no desserts and no smirking, and other people's parents crying just out of sight, but the inciting sins remained obscure to her even now. Nothing could have been as sinister as her young idea of sin, nor as elusive; she would have followed that curiosity anywhere. Her body prickled to know what caused others shame.

Nearly one hundred brothers and sisters had floated in the Great Exclusion, she now knew. They were kept from Meetings, and so kept from singing, and worked silently among church members in good standing and idle talk. They could not shake hands nor come on their knees in public prayer. Should any have died in exclusion, their souls would sink without petition.

One asked for the Great Exclusion as one asked for baptism: in public and in despair. There was something powerful, they were ever assured, about standing before the gathered Brotherhood and confessing failure. But like everything else worth curiosity, catharsis was addictive.

Many felt more comfortable in exclusion than they had in good standing with the Brotherhood. It was a release from dull talk at snack time and the delusion of community, a solemn holiday from the body of Christ. As children, they had imitated the grown-ups and played exclusion as a game. Even then, temporary isolation hurt wonderfully.

Like baptism, exclusion swept communities. "Exclusion-industrial complex," said Ruth to Alan, after a Brotherhood in which three Shalom requested the big exclusion and were granted the little one, for a noisome, failed late-night goat prank. From the safe vantage of middle age, Ruth regarded external exclusion with boredom.

"We don't need no stinkin' exclusion," said Alan. It meant nothing but that he was in a good mood.

It was Sunday approaching noon, and habit commanded that families gather, allot children, and fan out hiking until afternoon snack. Although the Feders had historically avoided vigor, that Sunday they offered to push blind Oma Hedwig all the way around the Bluebell Trail.

IN A WINDOWLESS ROOM BENEATH THE MEETING HALL, SIX SISters staffed Documents, carrying out the elders' directives, trafficking in holy obedience the worldly evidence of community life. Passports, visas, travel itineraries, death certificates, and all other manner of lubricating paperwork necessary for a member's transfer. As an internal organ, Documents was the spleen, offered Ruth to polite confusion.

Some families moved frequently, while others knew only one home. As a child, Ruth had dreamt of the Badlands, a grainy, low-contrast realm of sleet tornadoes and Hutterisch dirges to which her family might be any day sent forever. In the steady decades since their last split with the Western Colonies, however, entire generations had been raised without the terror of spontaneous transfer to the West. Now, Gretel merely, recurrently, claimed that any Dorf was better than the privation of Hazel Vale. She had on good and insistently anonymous authority that Australian Dorfs had cocoa powder in the Help Yourself room; she pleaded to be sent.

Ruth knew her nature disqualified her from a job so consequential. Documents sisters were sober and incurious, bored by the lives they changed. To most but Ruth, any job with food or babies was preferable to desk bondage. Still, for the community to persist in perpetual roil against complacency, these sisters would stare at screens and file in triplicate.

Summonses to move appeared, like late library book notices and anonymous encouragement, in one's mail-room cubby, faxed from foreign elders and always signed with love. Typically these invitations simply announced the date of anticipated arrival. The more pretext offered, the less persuasive it became, and even children knew to suspect a Shalom sister transferred suddenly and to a specific task; the engagement Love Meal followed swiftly, the lie buried in joy.

Ruth could not recall one single unmarried sister among those chosen to work in Documents, and realized with rare awe that the elders had intended it so.


ONE DAY AFTER EASTER, SHE COLLECTED THE WRAPPED BASKET from Stores and brought it home with the week's provisions. It stayed under their bed until Alan left to brush his teeth; while he was in the bathroom she carried it into the darkened living room and set it at her place at the table.

She had, since childhood, been able to transport herself outside the borders of her body. It was easiest in bed, where she could lie very still and imagine that her hands were tiny pincers or baseball mitts. She was deep and cozy in her brain, and nearly fifty years old, growing and shrinking while Alan snored beside her.

In the morning she opened her birthday basket and made the annual threat to compose a meal from its contents. Stores had given her a jumbo Toblerone bar, water crackers, mustard, two boxes of Lady Grey tea, a set of watercolor pencils, and lily of the valley–scented hand cream labeled "not for individual sale." From Wheat-haven, Rose sent a card. From Gretel, Ruth received a portrait of a horse, a blatantly repurposed old art assignment.

The morning passed without opportunity to inflict her disappointment. She was sung to at snack, sung to at lunch, and subhuman with exhaustion by midafternoon; she was asleep at her desk when Morina Hauptmann called from the mail room to alert her of a package, and already she wanted to set it on fire.

But she had hours to go before night, and, birthday or no, committed to rejoice in the Lord always; so to the mail room she trundled. Perhaps it was a surprise from Alan. Perhaps Billy Yoder, from back at ICC, had been given delayed, divine grace, confessed Christ, and mailed her a box of bonbons in gratitude.

It was a mild, yellow-lit afternoon, and a third-grade class gathered leaves in the Rook Woods. They sang "Happy Birthday" when she passed but she could not blame them.

It was a gift from Jamie, a potted rose he must have ordered on the internet, and Ruth began to cry. She was ashamed at the depth of her ingratitude. Everything happened so much.

GREETING CARDS, LIKE GROUND BEEF, HAD AT LEAST THREE LIVES, and it would be immoral to extract any less pleasure from them. The Scriptures clearly implied that all good things could be deferred, diluted, or—better yet—not desired at all.

Each Dorf printed original cards at Christmas and Easter. The prevailing style was labored realism, the palette murky and tempera based. An unindividuated collective of Shalom girls did the painting. Working as one body and without ego, they explored the difference between accuracy and artistry, gridding passionately—was it plagiarism or reverence? In any case, box by box, the ethnic infant or wildflower tableau moved from printout to canvas, and then back to printout, on mid-weight glossy cardstock with an inexplicable odor bought in tonnage at vast discount in 2003.

Cards were distributed like any other staple provision, a dozen per woman per household (Shalom boys received: none). In first circulation, cards went untouched, merely holding separate correspondence on lined paper. In theory, things could go on like this

forever, but convention dictated that in second sending the card itself bear text. The greetings were meaningless but permanent, and,
should the card merit a third trip around the wider Dorf, it would
need to be cut up and pasted detail-side down onto complementary
construction paper.

Ruth destroyed many Sunday afternoons in her shoebox of re-
cycled cards. This was doubly indulgent, for she never sent the cards
she made, knowing nobody prepared for a collage of identical lambs
gliding through a sunset, morons all.

ABORTION AND MURDER AROUSED IN RUTH NO MORE OR LESS DIS-
tress than any other structural incoherence. By all accounts, death
was enviable but God discouraged it.

She noted with suspicion those who wept at theoretical death.
Adelheid Wollmann crying in description of Anne Frank was a
performance of implausible sympathy. What did it matter that God
recalled some sooner than others? Blessed unsuffering experiments,
these early deaths. Adelheid Wollmann had probably not wept at
the knowledge of Ruth's weeping.

What was missing in Ruth's heart that her only intuitive reaction was disgust?

Carol, describing an addled custard as "schlurpy," caused Ruth
more distress than Pol Pot and Biafra combined.

SWEPT, DUST MOPPED, SPOT-CLEANED, AND WET MOPPED DAILY,
the Redwood House still smelled vile. Edeltraud Ayler was the first

to admit it, and in so doing self-admonished; surely hers was the offending family, she pled. Edeltraud had married in from the Colonies and kept immaculate house, so surely hers was not; this left the Feders, the Kesslers, and the Grumbachs.

The Grumbachs, whose very name suggested race cars or burrowing animals, were a family of six boys and so the most probable cause. In community euphemism, they were a lively family. Their youngest, Obediah, once challenged the Brotherhood during Family Meeting to tell him how much poop a bird weighed. Ruth could easily imagine the Grumbach boys harboring a turd.

But ripening, it became clear the smell originated on the second floor, exonerating all but the Kesslers and Feders. "Is it I?" Ruth asked Petra Kessler. Petra did not laugh at this or any other potentially heretical jollity, but merely offered that she planned to do a thorough clean that afternoon and would gladly buff their shared hallway. Ruth thought about chastening, then chastity belts. She lay on the floor of her living room while Petra buffed next door.

But neither buffing nor not buffing fixed the problem. Gretel's labored mouth-breathing was only a joke for a few days; soon the whole second floor smelled so richly of death that even Alan complained. Finally, Ruth defaulted to guilt and cleaned her own home like a newlywed. She emptied and scrubbed their cupboards, snaked the faucet, and even peered behind the radiator using a mirror borrowed from Dental. There was no smell in the reflection.

Her own bedroom smelled of itself so she did not suspect it. This left only Gretel and Carol's shared room, a conclusion with great risks; why would either girl lie about harboring putrefaction? When she should have worked, Ruth investigated the girls' room and solved one mystery while launching another. She stood in her socks on Carol's desk and unscrewed the ventilation duct, behind which rotted a puddle of former rodent and a pornographic magazine dated 2004. Ruth absorbed the majority of the former into the latter and put it in the trash, which, though nearly empty, she double-bagged and buried in the dumpster behind Stores. She could not call her son to tell him how little she cared about his sins.

HER SECOND HOTEL STAY, HER SECOND CRUCIBLE.

She could not situate buffet breakfasts on the moral continuum: Christlikeness produced bounty, but no guidance for encountering it. Ruth, in the lobby restaurant of the Wyndham Sault Ste. Marie, elected to panic. She, Alan, Curtis, and Annaliese Becker were there overnight on the pretext of Meeting and praying with a Quaker colloquium. In the van Ruth had erred in wondering aloud whether Quakers might love peace more than they loved Christ, which she'd read somewhere and liked the sound of. No one responded. Alan observed a dead hedgehog on the side of the road, and Curtis shared some conjecture on whether a hedgehog could still eject quills postmortem. Ruth pickled in shame.

They convened at six the next morning and lurked amid the lobby ferns until a bashful, vested waiter seated them early. The breakfast buffet seemed to Ruth extravagant, but Alan explained that it would be their only meal that day and so, for $19.95 each, a mandatory gluttony.

In her first pass she partook boldly of the exotics: an entire bowl of kiwi and raspberries gleaned from the fruit cornucopia, flaps of peameal bacon, and two cantilevered Danishes. Too late, she noticed the omelet station where Annaliese was interfering. In her second pass she attained her own omelet, a bowl of Frosties, and three packets of powdered cocoa that she hid first under her napkin and then under an empty plate. Returning from her third voyage she was embarrassed to see the cocoa naked at her place, its cover bused. She avoided all the eyes at her table.

In early fall the Gurkha dancers came to Hazel Vale.

The trouble began before the dancing could, when seven women walked single file into the Meeting Hall stage with bare feet and bellies. Most brothers knew to look away, into their laps or at the Gothic script across the cross beam. If, in the name of Jesus, they had victory over demons, surely they could conquer surprise flesh. The high school boys blushed in a crew-cut clot toward the back. Ruth, grateful for any spectacle that favored her sex, stared with impunity as dancers padded into line. She had never before seen so much skin in real life, nor did it now clarify the attraction of men to female bodies. Lust left Ruth alone.

The community faced seven soft milk-tea bellies. Dieter Grumbach, frantic at the AV cart, hit play, and the music began at a volume calibrated for the community's hearing aids. To diabolical keening the Gurkhas began to dance.

Markus Hauptmann and Simon Ayler stood and walked from the room. Brother by brother, the Meeting Hall vacated of men. Even drowsing Johnny Wollmann was wheelchaired out and parked beneath the eaves, where he awoke and smiled vaguely at the exodus.

In the Meeting Hall only women and children remained.

With Dieter fled, the AV cart was unsupervised, and so the Gurkha songs played on as the dancers ceased undulation. Two of them, attributing the exodus to danger, made to follow the men out of the Meeting Hall; only Edeltraud Ayler's bodily interception kept them contained. A quick sisters quorum, seven Kelly-green table runners, and grace brought the performance back under Christ's gaze. Brothers reentered, eyes up. Dieter soothed his cart and started again at track one. Though the performance defied comprehension, all could be trusted to confirm that the Gurkha dancers had been quite *interesting*.

Under scrutiny, the details of the invitation process revealed a lack of diligence; the simplest internet search would have spared everyone.

"I always imagined Nepal was quite cold," said Carol the day after, in morning flight from station to station across the Shop floor. Ruth, silent at her drill press, pondered the word *always*; was Carol obsessed by Nepal?

"All I know is, I certainly couldn't climb Mount Everest in one of those costumes."

CERTAIN BOOKS WERE NOT PERMITTED IN THE COMMUNITY AT all: smut, exploitative violence, mystic and demonic works. Others were in private circulation, passed from household to household after children were in bed: a controversial bestseller in which the Trinity was recast with God as a Black woman, for example. Still others were simply edited with a straight razor before they appeared on the library shelves. For his fourteenth birthday, Jamie had asked for the book of all the cutout pages.

In the end, though, it was not prurience but suffering that tempted the young people. The memoir of a young Catholic nun, captured, tortured, and raped while serving in Nicaragua, gained troubling popularity among the Shalom girls. They envied her martyrdom; such graphic piety, in such foreign hands, was surely nobler Christian service than buffing the Meeting Hall. In Meetings, the bolder among them asked to be sent on mission. In private, they imagined a suffering so joyful that even their captors could be won for Christ.

The book itself, even relieved of its most gruesome pages, was alarming. Ruth read it with one eye shut against the violence, and gave up before the rescue and rote inspiration of the last chapter. In old age she found simple evil boring.

Mission requests were quietly deferred and then denied, and eventually the Shalom as a whole came to repent for the arrogance of their fervor. They asked for and were gladly granted forgiveness. Ruth agreed: God's will was worked out in humble acts of service and adult sanity. To die having buffed the Meeting Hall was to die to the self that sought any grander life.


Two decades of polite correspondence with Merle convinced Ruth that certain hearts were known only to God. By mutual but tacit contract, they dwelled on topics in which neither had interest: rainfall, stories of everyday heroism from the local news, birds. Every Christmas, Merle sent the Feders a gift as inscrutable as her letters: a box of cherry liqueurs for the adults and a reliably perturbing gift for Gretel.

When Gretel had turned nine, Merle sent her a box of black ballpoint pens. The next year it was a set of plastic luggage tags from a bankrupt airline. The year after that it was a woman's size medium poncho of black chenille.

Merle's gifts challenged Ruth's confidence in mothering; while Gretel was frankly and ever more insulted by each present, her ingratitude was unacceptable. Thanking Merle for that year's Christmas parcel, Ruth mentioned that Gretel had of late caught the mania for cleaning and was disposing of household objects with fascistic vigor. Merle was impervious to hints: her next letter contained for Gretel a sheet of Easter Seals bearing Merle's own name and address.

RUTH'S CALLING CAME LATE BUT LOUDLY. AT FIFTY-ONE, SHE began drawing birthday announcements on the Shop whiteboard.

Her first was a Snoopy with balloons for Kyongguk Kim, thirty-two. Two days later, Tobias and Bertina Schmidt's thirteenth anniversary occasioned a new announcement, mountain laurels draped across their names in bubble letters. For Virginia Kupp she drew a portrait generous in its elision: "Happy eighteenth to the girl between the dimples!"

The Shop's stock of dry-erase markers spontaneously self-depleted until Annaliese began locking it in the office, so every morning Ruth had to request and return the key twice. She loved this obstruction; it added minutes to her private diversionary bee dance.

While her better brothers and sisters toiled, Ruth stood on a chair in an empty room and drew cartoons.

Her technique was honed by a limiting palette of four colors, one black marker, and spit. All women received ski-jump noses and eyelashes, and Ruth crossed their arms when she didn't feel like doing hands. Men were harder; many of Ruth's looked like the same broad-shouldered infant in different plaid shirts. She wrote limericks to distract from the worst pictures.

Only once did she err to the point of censorship. Beside her picture of Dieter Grumbach, Hazel Vale's notably fretful Steward, she had written *Jesus sez "Do not worry"—Matthew 6:25*. By snack, the text read *Happy birthday!* in Carol's cramped hand.

GRAVE DECISIONS CAME BY FOLDED NOTE, NEWS BY LETTER, AND gossip in person. Still, there were times when phone calls were necessary, so at great expense the community maintained direct lines between all the Dorfs. Phones were strategically installed to discourage misuse; each was shared between three families, equidistant from closable doors, so that all conversations must remain hallway-appropriate. The directory, a copy of which was laminated and pinned beside each phone, neatly summarized priorities on the Dorf: the Servants, Steward, and each work department had a dedicated line.

All inter-Dorf and outgoing calls went through switchboard. Just as Shalom girls were regularly challenged to serve against their strengths in landscaping projects, Shalom boys were often assigned switchboard duty, where they had to sit still and incurious for four hours a shift.

In theory, phone use was unlimited and unmonitored; the leadership knew that nothing induced rationing like abundance. After Rose was moved to Wheathaven, Ruth had waited three months before phoning. As switchboard attempted to locate her daughter, she scanned her list of Things to Mention, a document begun and abandoned the week after Rose left. Time encrypted her ambitions; the past Ruth who wanted to mention *limerick for Dad, fiction question/ morality,* and *brown snakes???* had died to Ruth of the present, now startled from her séance by some dear Shalom boy offering to put her through to the Wheathaven Laundry.

Ruth accepted his offer, but it was not Rose patched through. "Rose can't talk right now," explained a voice in Wheathaven. Behind it Ruth heard tumble drying and laughter.

"Is she behaving herself?"

The voice curled with complicity. "Last week she cut bangs into her hair."

Though not in and of themselves forbidden, deviating haircuts forebode.

"The horror, the horror," she muttered. But she did not worry. Rose, with her childlike faith and gummy smile, would sooner die than disobey, and Ruth knew the voice was just trying to scare her.

ESTHER SCHOLL, STILL LIVING IN GRACEFIELD AND ADJUNCT TO A Korean family without grandparents on-Dorf, desired her family and chameleons for her eightieth birthday. It was not a new desire, but at eighty she could openly request what she had only privately desired at seventy-nine. Flights were booked, a van requisitioned, the appropriate supervisors alerted, and the Feders took a day-trip to the Elmvale Jungle Zoo.

Gretel was in a foul mood, and knew no other adjective for the duration of the journey. The van, the egg salad sandwiches packed for lunch, and creatures in captivity were all "foul." She frowned out the window for a few miles and then began picking at her skin in the reflection.

"Speaking of foul," Alan said.

"Another Foul Day: The Gretel Feder Story," Ruth said. Esther knitted, oblivious.

Admission to the zoo cost forty-six dollars per adult, which Alan produced from his belt bag with labored formality. Ruth could not imagine any experience worth forty-six dollars, especially when the gift shop sold photo postcards for two dollars each. She knew her husband would forbid her from even browsing. He said something distantly humorous and the ticket agent smiled. With no evidence but rare faith, Ruth believed it was days such as these that anticipated Christ's Resurrection. She had finally read Revelation, and for all the beasts, remembered best the description of a Heaven defined by the nouns it lacked: death, mourning, sorrow, tears. A modest facility in which mixed species could rest together without histrionics. Wearily wearily down the stream; labeled paid zoogoers, Esther and the Feders entered the Amphibian Pavilion.


FEW PLUMBED VANITY WITH THE DEFTNESS OF THE HIGH SCHOOL girls. Their lives were devised to discourage embodiment: like all women in the community, they worked in long skirts, slept in long

flannels, and transitioned between the two under a bell-shaped
modesty garment even while alone. Their faces were medievally
bare. And yet even upholstered and naked they defied.

They varied the width between mandated double plaits. First
the trend was to plait them close together, then wide apart, revealing tender scalps. They cuffed their short-sleeve blouses and let
their skirts down to hazardous lengths. Curtis Becker, both principal of the high school and father to two of its leading seditionaries,
wept before the Brotherhood in summary of the situation.

This had the flavor of Hitler's youth movement, announced one
older single sister. The high school girls were seeking power over
one another, not to speak of their male classmates; the Brotherhood
could not ignore the sin beneath the frivolity. Pair by pair, parents
stood to confess remission, vowing to make a new start in their
hearts and homes. Vera Wollmann, whose Sophie and Irini were
technically implicated but dim beyond concern, wondered if she
even deserved to call herself a mother. How did it feel to be Vera's
husband, standing with her before the microphone, declaring such
doubt? Pete Wollmann was a lean blank Colony refugee and no one
would ever know.

Ruth felt conspicuous in her silence but waited for Alan to rise
for confession. They were the last high school parents to speak, and
the litany of failure was plainly exhausted. Alan took the microphone from its stand; coughed; lifted the hand holding Ruth's to
scratch his chin.

"We should be the last family to cast stones," he said finally. "I
know Gretel is responsible for a lot of what the high school is quote
unquote experiencing right now."

Ruth's brain flared with vague, protective lies.

"But I have to ask myself, why is it my daughter's job to protect the high school boys from looking at her? Modesty is a two-way street, if that makes sense." She felt entirely persuaded by what she thought he was saying. Alan coughed again. "I don't know, it just seems weird to me, or what?"

They sat down, sang four evening songs, and then from the kitchen oblivious Shalom poured forth to serve mulled wine and cold cuts.

FOR CERTAIN YEARS RUTH WORKED ONLY WITH HER HUSBAND, supporting him in Fulfillment until again fit for those unmarried to her. She could come and go as she pleased, for Alan never had any tasks both worthwhile and safe from her caprice; cheerful, she made mischief, and mournful, she destroyed. Alan was never cross with her, but nor did he indulge his wife at the expense of his work. The three flat screens on his standing desk (the fourth iteration of a design that had possessed him since high school) provided a faceted mirror in which to observe his wife's activity, and she, at her own screen, could see him; the arrangement was at least equitable. Alan often reasoned with her in these terms: his job was to manage and refine delivery of the community's products; hers was to stay alive. He paced and grunted into his headset. She doodled, wrote poetry, and printed *Garfield* and *Peanuts* cartoons from the internet. She never lingered online, though she desperately wanted a few hours, unseen by God and Alan, to search.

The Fulfillment office was part of a warren of beige compartments beside the Shop floor. When the snack bell rang, all in the building joined the Shop crew for a respite of coffee, tea, and murmuring.

Shop snack attendance was a stipulation of Ruth's position working for Alan. "What kind of monster makes his wife spend fifteen minutes in the company of people who love her?" he would ask; if Ruth responded, it was only to name whichever mythological beast came to mind. He sat with the men and refused to acknowledge her until the work bell rang at eleven.

Sometimes she felt capable and sat with the sewing sisters, a sensible cabal who tended to discuss what might be for lunch. More often she joined the teenage Shop brothers, who had nothing to say to one another, let alone Ruth, and let her lurk in their midst like a potted geranium.

"What did you learn today?" Alan always asked on their return to the office.

"Heck is other people," she typically responded, and recited the lunch menu if she'd heard it.

RUTH WAS LATE FOR LUNCH, AND ENTERED THE MEETING HALL just as all eyes were cast down for the prayer. She watched from the door to see who would peek, and was unsurprised to count Gretel among the disobedient. The high schoolers were expected to sit with their families at community meals, and Gretel's catatonic grimace was clearly intended for Alan, who sat across from her with head bowed.

Ruth waited until the Austeilers began swirling to join her

family at their preferred table in the far corner of the room. Gretel, in constant pursuit of cause for disgust, inspected her fork in the sunlight. Alan, voluble and oblivious, explained why the Kyoto Protocol had been a farce.

She could hear his good mood and needed no explanation beyond what lay in front of him on the table: a plate of fried chicken and the latest issue of *The Economist*, to which the Dorf maintained one subscription for circulation among its more worldly brothers. A drumstick pinched in three fingers, Alan inscribed a circle in the air—a gesture toward "the neoliberal contingent," she gathered—but paused when she sat down beside him.

"Sleeping beauty awakes!" he said to Gretel, who was peeling her own drumstick into shreds. To Ruth: "You get some rest?"

She had already missed two mornings of work this week, subject to the miserable private gravity that kept her pinned in bed. It was rarely sleep; this morning she had been thinking about ratios. The number of things she could accomplish in one day, for example, would always be less than the number of things she could not accomplish—she would always fail to do far more than she did. Likewise, her sins of omission defied enumeration: each time she withheld laughter from Alan, every moment she spent bored, all the human suffering she could not metabolize. These sins overlapped and ran together and multiplied when examined. Her sins of commission, by contrast, were measly, occasional.

Although—and this was the line of thinking that made her late to lunch—the whole taxonomy of sin was extrapolation from the Bible's limited list. Ruth could not fathom temptation to most prohibited things. She thought herself prone to covetousness until learning that it meant only desire for married men, not novels and day-trips to Sudbury. Killing, bearing false witness, adultery, theft: flag football might as well have been forbidden, so little did these things bear on her soul.

Ruth knew herself to be a sinner, with a certainty that she lacked as a Christian, a woman, or a human. She knew it was sinful to sit on the edge of her bed, curtains drawn and binder-clipped together against whatever late morning had to offer, trying to deflate a wart on her knee with a dull needle, thinking critically of the Bible. But why? She had asked as much in letters to Servant's wives for decades now. The few who wrote back wrote of other things.

She noticed that Alan's mode had changed from discursive broadcast to dialogue, and then realized he had been talking to her.

"Mom? Ruth?"

She bought some time with a coughing spell, then nodded at him.

"Just making sure that was deep thought and not a seizure."

She nodded again, and finally thought to put food on her plate. The platter of chicken had been emptied, was now refilled with bones and greasy twists of napkin; it was unlikely the kitchen would provide seconds. Ruth gestured for Gretel to slide her the bowl of carrot sticks.

"Anything interesting?" asked Alan.

It took a moment for her to place the question. "Just wondering what's for dinner."


BROTHER OH WAS GETTING MARRIED. THE BROTHERHOOD COULD and did thank only the Heavens. Though he wrote his proposal in

Korean and memorized its translation phonetically, the Spirit moved him to go off script. "Sister Brigid," he shouted, too excited to wait for the microphone moving toward him from the other side of the circle. "You are loving Jesus so much!"

Dear Brigid Dettweiler stood from her seat and grinned back at him. She was half Hutterite, with treacherously high cheekbones and narrow eyes that looked like ventilation. Five years his senior, Brigid had long enjoyed the community's structured consolation for older, unmarried women; she was excused from Shalom activities and given a digital camera with which to photograph her exquisite orchids. And now God would make her a wife! A vile fraction of Ruth wondered whether she'd have to return the camera.

Brigid was a reader and a writer, of a wholesome intellect piqued by truth rather than novelty. What had she written to Brother Oh? What had they understood of one another that made each so eager to serve and supplicate? Despite her fondness for him, Ruth could not imagine marriage to Brother Oh, but she could rarely even imagine marriage to her own husband.

Brigid moved across the room to stand beside Brother Oh. Every present wife recognized in her face the giddy anticipation of obedience; Brigid was already folding his socks in her heart. They would, in time, need one another entirely, for solitude was as easy to forget as springtime in the winter.

Ruth reflected on her own marriage, and concluded that its innards were exactly as complex and boring as anyone else's. Daily exposure to one person leveled all external qualifiers, for better and worse; inside of a marriage, even Brother Oh might learn to sneer.

RUTH AND ALAN HAD BEEN SENT TO EDENDALE FOR THE WEEK-end to attend the wedding of Alan's niece, a contrivance only in retrospect, when suddenly they were granted permission to visit Jamie. They left after breakfast for the Amtrak Hiawatha to Chicago; Ruth, for want of a pocketbook, carried her reading glasses and a tributary Snickers bar in the canvas pouch that usually held her toiletries. While she was sobered by anxiety, Alan grew even chattier, entrapping three successive passengers in discussion of: Japanese factory efficiency theory, American Sign Language, the necessity of community, and the frequency with which avowed atheists—here he dipped his head conspiratorially—professed Christ with their deeds if not their lips. Ruth disliked the word *lips* on his. They passed a sign for Kalamazoo.

Alan and his third victim, a young raw-scalped soldier with a duffel bag clamped between his thighs, were deep in agreement on society's need for obedience.

"What do you think is the most popular syllable in the world?" she interrupted.

She found her question charming and repeated it. "Including babies, but not including animals."

Alan and the soldier could not be distracted. Ruth thought of Jamie and tried to launch herself into a future off the train.

They were to meet their son at the Information desk at Union Station after eighteen months apart. They were nearly half an hour early and vigilantly waited, demanding that each thin, dark-haired figure resolve into Jamie as it approached. Each failed them, until finally, five minutes early, one did not.

He was pretty, Ruth thought without reflection. What had once flashed as mischief now radiated as beauty: her son. She wanted everyone in Union Station to feel his tremor as he hugged her, to know that this young man with a complicated haircut loved this old woman in a headscarf and plaid. Jamie released her and shook his father's hand.

At Subway he told them about his creative writing class and his neighborhood and the train he took from one to the other twice a day. They ate sandwiches bought with money from the Steward; three identical meaningless sandwiches she would later describe repeatedly when asked about visiting Jamie. Better to discuss the corned beef—called pastrami in Chicago, she'd add quizzically—than how it felt to realize that her son belonged outside the church.

Alan left to find the station bathroom, and Ruth tried to summon eighteen months of mischief in his absence.

"You look happy, Mama," Jamie interrupted. Her account of a Saturday supper skit withered, irrelevant, as overhead a recording announced delays on the Blue Line. Jamie took the Blue Line; every weekday morning his soul sat utterly anonymous while she sang and moped in community. Behind him she saw Alan approach, gesturing at his watch.

Panic blunted her wit. "I am," she told him, before and after a pause. "I think."

"Yes, you do," Jamie said.

# Acknowledgments

Thank you Mom, Dad, and Cam.

Thank you Gabe, Emma, n+1; thank you Teddy, Lorin, and everyone at *The Paris Review*.

Thank you Jim and Seren.

Thank you Rebecca and Delia at Riverhead, and Bobby at Transworld.

Thank you Abby, Alice, Amanda, Ani, Anna, Annabel, Brodsky, Cherra, Colleen, Dana, Elaine, Emily, Erin, Genny, Hannah, Izzy, Katie, Lauren, Lucy, Maggie, Mary, Miriam, Molly, Nora, Olivia, Phoebe, Rachel, Rebecca, Rudnick, Sheila, and Tara.